PLAGUE YEAR

Stephanie S. Tolan

FAWCETT JUNIPER • NEW YORK

For Frances Carpenter and Barriss Mills,
teachers who made a difference

RLI: $\dfrac{\text{VL 5 \& up}}{\text{IL 6 \& up}}$

A Fawcett Juniper Book
Published by The Ballantine Publishing Group
Copyright © 1990 by Stephanie S. Tolan

www.ballantinebooks.com

Library of Congress Catalog Card Number: 89-13605

ISBN 0-449-70403-3

This edition published by arrangement with William Morrow and Company, Inc.

First Ballantine Books Edition: December 1991

OPM   13   12

ACKNOWLEDGMENTS

Thanks to Carl Heiner, principal of Waterford/Halfmoon High School, Waterford, New York, and Janet Lynch of Albany County Social Services for their assistance.

CHAPTER 1

I MAY HAVE been the first person in Ridgewood to see Bran Slocum. It was the first Saturday in October, about seven o'clock in the morning. The sun was turning the edges of the hills outside of town orange, and some wisps of mist were still rising from the damp ground. I was up and outside at that ungodly hour, pounding the sidewalk and sweating in the chilly air, mainly because of Molly Pepper.

I'd been dating Kristin Matthis since about the middle of the summer, and when Kristin made the cheerleading squad, Molly, who takes better care of my social life than I do, pointed out that it wasn't reasonable for a cheerleader to date Watson the Wimp. If I wanted to keep Kristin, I had to become a jock. The problem was that I'm tall and skinny (''free of excess body fat,'' Molly said) and have these really long arms and legs. I'm not crazy about heavy body contact, so football was out. It was the wrong season for basketball even if I could shoot baskets, which I can't.

But I can run. I'm not fast, but I have terrific endurance. Once I get started, I can run practically forever. So Molly insisted I try out for the cross-country

1

track team, and I did, just to keep her off my back. To my surprise, I made it. There have to be at least five runners on a cross-country team if the school wants to compete officially and get ranked. Only four of the guys who tried out were fast, and none of them could go as far as I could, so Coach Morelli took me on in the hope that he could find some way to increase my speed. That's why I was out that Saturday morning. Coach had given me a stopwatch to time my runs. I was supposed to try to take a few seconds off my time every day, running the same course.

You've heard of that movie, *The Loneliness of the Long-Distance Runner*? I've never seen it, but the title's right on. Long-distance running isn't the kind of thing you do in groups. I mean, who else in their right mind would leave a nice, warm bed and an X-rated dream about Miss October to put on some holey sweats and run through the empty weekend-morning neighborhoods of Ridgewood, New York?

I'd been running half an hour, and I hadn't seen a single person except an old lady who was standing on her porch in her bathrobe, waiting for her pug dog to finish his business in her rhododendrons. That's why I particularly noticed when a cab drove past me, going real slow, and pulled up in front of a tired-looking, aluminum-sided two-story house down almost where Larch Street ends at the back of Ridge Lawn Cemetery.

My route takes me through the cemetery because the gravel road is better for running than sidewalks, if you watch out for the ruts and dips, and because it looks terrific in there in the fall, when the leaves are changing. That's something you can't say about the

2

neighborhood in general. Or most of Ridgewood for that matter.

I kept on running toward the cab as its back door opened and somebody heaved a duffle bag out onto the sidewalk and then climbed out after it. He must not have heard me coming. He reached into the cab and grabbed a backpack, swung it over his shoulder, and then backed right into me, as I started to swerve to avoid the duffle.

In the moment it took to get my balance and avoid falling, I got a good look at him. He seemed about my age, shorter than me by a couple of inches, but built better, with good shoulders and a tough-looking body. His hair was an ordinary sort of brown, but so long he'd tied it into a ponytail that hung a good six inches down the back of his jeans jacket. He had two rolled red and white bandannas tied around his neck. And he had an earring in one ear. You couldn't miss it. It was a big gold hoop.

He grunted when we hit, and turned toward me, his face startled—scared. For just a minute, he was like an animal in the middle of the road when your headlights hit it, eyes wide and terrified. Then he blinked, and it was as if he'd slipped a mask on. His face went blank.

"Sorry," I muttered. He frowned at me. At least I think he was frowning at me. It was hard to tell. His right eye was off somehow, angled sort of over my shoulder, while the other seemed to bore into my forehead. His mouth was a straight, tight line. "Sorry," I said again, though it hadn't really been my fault.

Still frowning, he settled his backpack more firmly onto his shoulder and I turned away and started running again. I glanced back over my shoulder once, and saw a balding guy with a paunch come out of the house and start down toward the kid, who was paying the cab driver, and then I ran on.

By the time I was through the service gate and onto the cemetery's gravel road, I'd just about forgotten the whole thing, watching the coils of mist that were rising from among the headstones like anemic ghosts.

I'd been running through the cemetery every day, and I don't think I'd ever thought about the dead people. But that morning, I had a couple of second thoughts. When I came out the main gate and checked the stopwatch, I saw that I'd made it through in record time. Not great time for cross-country maybe, but great for me.

I found out Slocum's name and that he'd come to Ridgewood to stay when I got to school Monday morning. He was in my homeroom, and he got there late, because of having to go to the office first and get enrolled. Maybe it would have helped if he'd been there right at the bell like everybody else, so he wouldn't have had to make that solitary entrance, but with the way he looked, maybe not.

When the classroom door opened, Mrs. Campbell had just finished taking the roll and was reading off the morning announcements for the junior class. People were shifting around and whispering, the way they always do during homeroom, and a couple of the conscientious types were finishing up homework. But the minute Slocum came through the door, everybody stopped whatever they were doing and it got real quiet. People just stared.

Maybe back in the sixties there were guys at Ridgewood who wore their hair in ponytails. But not now. Some guys wear their hair pretty long, but they mousse it and let it hang sort of full and wavy over their shoulders. Most everybody else wears their hair like mine, short enough that even in a high wind, it doesn't move a whole lot. So the hair was one thing.

Then there were the scarves—and that earring. And the eye. He stood there in the doorway, his left eye looking at Mrs. Campbell, and the right seeming to stare out the window. His mouth was that hard, straight line and he had no expression on his face at all, as if he'd been carved out of stone.

The silence didn't last. As he walked over to Mrs. Campbell's desk to hand her his late pass and his enrollment card, Matt Singleton, who sits right in front of me, whispered that the guy ought to be wearing a dress to go with his hair and his earring. People who hadn't heard asked others, and pretty soon Matt's observation had made its way up every aisle.

Slocum turned and looked at the class when Mrs. Campbell pointed to an empty desk at the back of the second row, and everybody got a clear look at the eye that turned slightly out and up and seemed to move on its own.

"Oh, n-no!" Matt said, out loud this time, "P-P-Princess Charming has the evil eye." There were a few giggles.

"Matthew!" Mrs. Campbell said, pushing herself to a standing position behind her desk. "That's enough out of you. This is . . ." she glanced at the card in her hand. "This is Bran Slocum, and I want you all to make him welcome."

There was silence again for about two seconds. Bran Slocum stood looking out over the faces turned toward him, then sort of ducked his chin and started toward his seat, his backpack hanging off one shoulder. "Bran muffin," somebody behind me muttered, and laughter swept the room.

"Bran flake," someone else said.

"Class! Settle yourselves immediately!" Mrs. Campbell banged her roll book on the desk, but the laughter didn't stop.

"Raisin bran" was next, and then Matt let out a huge guffaw. *"Fruitful B-B-Bran!"* he shouted, and doubled over his desk. That did it. Anybody who hadn't laughed before was laughing now, me included.

"Class!" Mrs. Campbell said again, but she didn't have a chance of getting order now, and she knew it.

"Fruitful Bran," someone else repeated, and the laughter overwhelmed Mrs. Campbell's voice completely. She just gave up, and stood at the front of the room, reading the rest of the announcements into the din. I twisted around in my seat to see how Slocum was taking it, thinking how glad I was not to be in his position. I remembered that look I'd seen when I'd bumped into him. That moment of fear. But he just sat there, his mask in place, perfectly quiet except for one finger, tapping on the chipped Formica of his desk top.

The all-school announcements were made over the loudspeaker, and then the bell rang to end homeroom. Mrs. Campbell turned her back and began writing the assignment for her first-period class on the board as everybody grabbed their stuff and shoved out into the hall, talking and giggling. Everybody except Slocum, who stayed at his desk, probably waiting till we were all gone. I had a feeling, as I left,

6

that for as long as he was a student at Ridgewood High, he was going to be called Fruitful.

At lunch, when Kristin had left our table to go to a cheerleaders' meeting, Molly picked up her tray from the table where she usually sits and came to join me. I was surprised, because even though Molly and I are good friends, hardly anybody at school even knows about it. That's her doing, mostly.

I've known her all my life, or at least as long as I can remember. When we were little our parents spent a lot of time with each other, so we were together a lot. In grade school we were pretty much best friends.

It changed in junior high. That was when kids started paying a lot of attention to how people looked. And Molly wasn't pretty or cute. She was short and squat and had a plain face. When the other girls were getting figures, Molly wasn't. When the other girls started wearing makeup and paying lots of attention to clothes and hair, Molly didn't. She wore her dark hair straight and parted in the middle, and always dressed in jeans and oversized T-shirts or sweat shirts. Nick Bruno called her Goblin Girl one day, and the name stuck.

She started avoiding me in school. At first my feelings were hurt, but she went on calling me on the phone a lot, and we still did things together on weekends sometimes. She said we could stay friends, but there wasn't any point in both of us being unpopular. "If people get the idea that we're going together or something, you won't have a chance," she told me. And it didn't take me long to discover that things were easier for me if people didn't connect me with "Goblin Girl."

By the time we started high school, we both wanted

to keep things the way they were. It worked out pretty well for me. I got to keep Molly as a friend, which I wanted to do. But I could date other girls without having to worry about hurting her feelings. "You do the usual high school stuff for both of us," Molly said during our sophomore year. "If anything really interesting happens you can tell me all about it. That way, I won't miss anything, but I won't have to figure out how to change myself into somebody I'm not just to fit in." And she didn't change, either. She was a little taller, though not very much, and built more like a girl, but she still didn't wear makeup or worry about clothes. And she really didn't seem to mind that she didn't have much of a social life. She contented herself with overseeing mine.

"Have you seen him?" she asked that day, when she'd plunked her plastic tray down next to the remains of my peanut-butter-and-jelly-and-apple lunch.

"Who?"

"Slocum, of course. You think there's any other guy around here I'd be asking about?"

"Well—there's your crush on Dr. Towson."

"Oh, yeah. It's my fondest dream to marry an uptight, by-the-book, middle-aged high school principal. Have you seen Slocum?"

"In math, like you."

"I meant during lunch. Where is he?"

"How should I know? Maybe he brown-bags it like us poor folk. He could be eating outside by the fountain. Why?"

"Just wondered. 'Fruitful.' That is so disgusting." She flipped her hair behind her ears and took a bite of creamed corn. "I suppose you think hassling Slocum's just good, clean fun."

8

I gathered up my empty sandwich bag, apple core and juice box and stuffed them into the crumpled brown bag. "No, but a little teasing isn't going to kill him. He'll survive it, just like the rest of us. You survived 'Goblin Girl.' "

"Sure, but not everybody's as tough as me."

"What makes you think he'd even appreciate your concern? He's not exactly Mr. Personality." Just then I saw Bran Slocum come through the cafeteria doors. "Speak of the devil."

He was greeted by whistles and catcalls. "Hey, Fruitful!" somebody yelled. I recognized the voice—Nick Bruno, junior class loudmouth, middle line-backer on the football team and all-round jerk. "We don't have a faggot table yet, Fruitful. Why don't you start one?"

Slocum, a lunch bag in one hand and his backpack over his shoulder, didn't even turn his head in Nick's direction. He just walked, with a kind of disinterested slouch, toward an empty table in the corner.

Molly pushed her hair behind her ears again, put her milk carton into the empty segment on her tray, and stood up. "Let's go sit with him," she said.

"No, thanks. He's your project. Anyway, I told Kristin I'd see her after her meeting."

"Okay, okay. Don't let me interfere with young love. See you later." Molly picked up her tray and headed for Slocum's table.

"Looky there," Nick called out as Molly said something to Slocum and put her tray down across the table from him. "The Goblin Girl's a fag lover!" More catcalls and whistles from the guys at Nick's table.

I headed for the door, tossing my bag into the trash

9

can as I went. The last thing I heard before the doors swung shut behind me was Molly's voice with an edge to it that cut through all the cafeteria's usual background noise. "Lay off, scumbag."

I grinned. I didn't know about Slocum, but Molly could handle Nick Bruno.

CHAPTER 2

A COUPLE OF times that week I wondered what makes the Nick Brunos of the world do what they do. It's as if there's a trigger that sets them off. If you've got it, you're in trouble. If you don't, you're okay. Bran Slocum had it. And it wasn't only Nick Bruno that got set off. His buddies, Matt Singleton, Jerry Ritoni and Gordon Krosky, took their cue from him and went after Slocum any way they could. Besides that, other guys who wanted to get in good with Nick were busy imitating them.

By Tuesday, someone had pained "FAGGOT" in pink letters on Slocum's locker. The next day the word was spangled with gold glitter. He was bumped and jostled in the hall and sometimes crowded into the lockers. Once he was nearly pushed down the steps when Jerry Ritoni faked a fall behind him. And always the name Fruitful followed him, called out down the halls, whispered in class, chalked onto the blackboards in rooms where he had classes.

I didn't pay any of it much attention, because I had other things on my mind. Running was one. The more I ran, the better I liked it. I was getting faster. Coach Morelli told me that week that if I kept at it, I just

11

might have the makings of a marathoner. It's amazing what being good at something does for the way you feel about it. We had practice after school every day, but I was the only one on the team who got up and ran every morning, too. It wasn't just for the team. Running made me feel good.

Kristin was on my mind a lot, too. Molly had said I needed to be on a team if I wanted to keep on dating a cheerleader, and that's why I'd started with cross-country in the first place. But during football season, football was the sport all the cheering was for. The football team got to see the cheerleaders all the time—the squad practiced right by the field. The cross-country team hardly ever even ran at school. Except for an occasional speed trial on the track, we ran a course Coach had laid out through a state park south of town. So I didn't get to see much of Kristin after school.

Besides that, she was a sophomore and we didn't have any classes together. If it hadn't been for lunch, we would hardly have seen each other at all. And there's just so much romance you can get into a conversation in the cafeteria. We usually went to a movie or a party Saturday night, but that was starting to get old. Boring. I didn't feel the way I had when we started seeing each other in the summertime, and I didn't think she did either. Something needed changing.

There was a dance after the pep rally and football game on Friday night, and I was hoping that would at least break the routine. I was planning to take her in the old pickup truck that is Dad's and my sole transportation, and if the weather was nice, we were going to go off by ourselves instead of to a party afterwards. I thought we could take some food and blankets and have a sort of picnic in the back. But on Wednesday Dad announced that there was a craft fair in Vermont on Saturday, and he was taking his stuff over in the truck Friday night to get set up.

It wasn't the first time my dad's peculiar profession had made problems for me. In some ways it does that every day of my life, and if I let myself think about it too much, it would cause real trouble between us. So I try not to. He's a wood carver, and what he mostly carves are totem poles, sort of contemporary ones, and smaller sculptures he calls "house and garden totems." Sometimes he does them on commission, but mostly he does them on his own. There isn't a booming market for totems, so they fill up our garage, which is also his workshop, and our backyard, which looks like some kind of petrified zoo. Bears, mountain lions, owls, eagles, possums and raccoons stand alone or on each other's heads and stare out at the world beyond our back fence.

There's a sign in front of our house that says, James Watson, Totems and Wood Sculpture, which is supposed to bring customers. But the bottom line is there isn't much bottom line. So he works part-time, seven till two, for a printer he's known since they were both hippies together twenty years ago. This gives him afternoons and evenings to carve, but it also means that we live a very frugal life. I have to work at the grocery store weekends if I want to have any cash at all. Even taking Kristin to the movies every so often was always a strain on my budget.

My mom used to try to get him to take some other kind of job—some forty-hour-a-week, full-time job that would pay real money, so things wouldn't always

13

be so tough. She said he could still carve evenings and weekends. But carving isn't just something my dad likes to do. It's his mission in life, a philosophical, ideological thing I don't quite understand. Mom didn't either. She left him to marry a lawyer when I was ten. They let me choose, and I stayed with Dad because I couldn't stand the lawyer. I don't regret my choice, really, but it hasn't been easy.

Mom left her totem, a fox, behind. It still stands in the front hall with Dad's dove and my wolverine. When she left he was working on a pole that had all three of them together, but he never finished it. Dad says it wasn't just the carving and the money that drove her away. The trouble with their marriage was that foxes and doves don't make very good companions. That's an example of the way he thinks about totems.

I tried very hard to persuade Dad to let me use the truck Friday, pointing out that I needed it sometimes, too. I suggested he could leave for Vermont really early Saturday morning. He said I could have a car of my own the minute I had the money for it, but meantime, the truck was his, and his friend the printer was coming over to help him load on Friday afternoon. So I was scrambling to find wheels for Kristin and me, and that's another reason why Bran Slocum wasn't on my mind a lot that week.

He was, however, on Molly's mind. She'd taken him on as one of her rescue projects. Every day at lunch he'd sit at the same table, always alone, and every day Molly would go over and sit with him, ignoring the taunts of Nick and his gang. I'd glance over at them from time to time, and Molly was always talking as she ate. She has about a million different

14

interests, and she must have told Slocum about every single one of them that week, because she didn't seem to be getting much of anything back from him. Theirs weren't actually conversations. He just sat there, eating, occasionally glancing at her, in that disconcerting way that didn't quite connect.

The only thing really unusual about that first week of Bran Slocum's life at Ridgewood High was that by Thursday, with everyone gearing up for Friday's big pep rally and game and dance, the harassment still hadn't faded out.

As Slocum came out of his last-period class Thursday, Gordon Krosky tripped him, and Jerry Ritoni and Matt Singleton grabbed his backpack as he went down. They kept it away from him, tossing it back and forth between them while he just stood and watched, until they had to go to football practice. Then they took it with them and dropped it into a toilet in the locker room. Slocum, having said nothing the whole time, followed them, picked it up, slung it dripping over his shoulder and walked out. I was sitting there, putting on my running shoes, and as I watched him go, his back straight, his head up, that ponytail moving slightly with each step, I thought it couldn't go on much longer. Not even Nick and his goons could keep it up with so little reaction from their victim. Or so I thought.

Friday morning I still hadn't solved the problem of wheels. I'd asked Artie Weston, who was also on the track team, if I could borrow his beat-up Volkswagen, but he'd asked Cheryl Heroux to the dance, so he was using it himself. A couple of guys offered to let us double, but the whole point was for Kristin and me to get off by ourselves for a change, and maybe get a little spark back into the fading fire, so I turned them down. It looked as if to be alone together, Kristin and I were going to have to walk. I was sure Kristin was going to loathe and despise that idea.

Maybe that was why my morning run went so badly. I was wiped out a couple of blocks after I started. Every step seemed to send the pavement up through my legs, the jolt reaching clear to my brain. I couldn't get my breathing timed right, and I was slower than ever. Besides, it was colder than it should have been so early in October. My hands, my nose and my ears felt as if they were going to fall off, even while the rest of me was sweating.

When I came out of the cemetery and saw Molly, a stocking cap pulled down over her ears, walking Muttsy, the three-legged stray she'd adopted, I slowed to a walk and joined her.

"Don't break training for me," she said. "Muttsy and I are having a great time all by ourselves."

"Is this your subtle way of telling me to get lost?"

"Nope. I just don't want to be blamed if you get in trouble with Coach Morelli."

"No problem. He's crazy about me." Muttsy sniffed a tree trunk and squatted, balancing precariously. "Is the invalid all better?"

"Dad says she's fine. She just needs to get used to getting around without the leg." Molly's father is a veterinarian, and her mother is his nurse, so maybe it comes with her genes to be a pushover for a sad, furry face.

I blew on my hands and started running in place. "I've got to get inside and get warm. You want to come over for breakfast? Dad's probably gone to work by now."

"What've you got?"

"Good stuff. Juice and dry cereal. High-fiber, low-salt, low-sugar stuff all full of nuts and berries and twigs."

"What if I want waffles? Or Sugar Pops?" Molly punched my arm. "What happened to bacon and eggs and pancakes, anyway? Your dad used to make the most enormous breakfasts—"

I punched her back. "He still does. I didn't say Dad eats this stuff, I said we *have* it. I eat it. And it's what I'm offering you. It's good for you. Capital G good. Also easy."

A few minutes later, we were on our way up the gravel driveway that leads through a scraggle of hedge to the bungalow with the peeling yellow paint that is Dad's and my house. Molly brought Muttsy inside.

It was obvious that Dad had been up, fixed his breakfast and gone. The egg carton was sitting open on the stove, greasy paper towels were next to the frying pan, dirty dishes and the orange juice pitcher and the jumbled wreck of the newspaper littered the table. Our small black-and-white television was on to the "Today" show. Willard Scott, wearing some sort of a turban, was pointing to the northeast on his map and talking about a strong warming trend.

"Good," I said, getting out the cereal and a carton of milk, "it's too early to be so cold." Molly, who knew her way around our kitchen as well as I did, set out bowls and spoons. "Sorry about the mess," I said.

"Don't worry about it," she answered, clearing Dad's dishes to the sink. She dropped a bacon scrap onto the floor, and Muttsy pounced on it with the

17

agility of a panther. "I guess I can stop worrying about you," she said to her.

"That car wrecked her leg, not her head. She still recognizes bacon when she smells it."

"Only some things are worth the effort, I guess. You should see how hard it is for her to get up when she has to go out and it's raining!"

While we ate, the kitchen was quiet except for the gurgling of our sick old coffee pot and the low drone of the television. "How's the boyfriend?" I asked Molly, when I'd finished my cereal and drunk the rest of the milk out of my bowl.

"What boyfriend?"

"Don't play games with me, Molly Pepper. I've seen you at lunch with him every single day."

"Boyfriend is hardly the operative word," Molly said, frowning. "He's not the most communicative person I've ever met."

"I'm sure you more than make up for that. So, what's he like?"

She shook her head and finished her orange juice. "It's funny, David, but Bran's different. Really different."

"Yeah. That's his whole problem. He could at least cut his hair."

"I don't mean the way he looks. I mean the way he *is*. You know what Bruno and his gang have been doing. He doesn't react. He doesn't get mad, he doesn't get upset. It's as if he's above it all. Or beyond it."

"Nobody's beyond that kind of thing," I said.

Muttsy whined, and Molly put her bowl, with a little milk in the bottom, on the floor for her. "I've been trying all week to figure out what it is about

Bran, and I can't. He's just—still. That's a good word for it. *Still.*"

"He hasn't had a chance to get a word in edgewise. Every time I've seen the two of you together, you've been the one doing the talking."

"He talks. Sometimes. As long as you don't ask direct questions. Anyway, it isn't about talking or being quiet. That's not what I mean. It's something about his whole self—who he is. He's just *still*." She sat for a moment, staring off into space. Molly does this from time to time, and you just have to wait her out. "Remember what I'm telling you," she said, after a bit. "There's something special about Bran Slocum. You'll see."

"Right." It sounded to me as if Molly was falling for the guy. I should have been happy for her. I had Kristin, now Molly would have Bran. I should have been happy, but for some reason, I wasn't. I wondered if I might be jealous, but dismissed the thought. It was probably just that I was used to knowing Molly only had me. That wasn't really jealousy, was it? "I've got to take a shower," I said, getting up. "If you wait, I'll walk you over to your place."

She checked her watch. "Okay, but we don't have much time. Tell you what. You walk me home, and I'll drive us to school. Then you can keep the keys and take my car for your date with Kristin."

I just looked at her.

"Well, don't you want it?"

"Of course I want it. You think I'm nuts?"

"Slow, maybe, never nuts. Hurry up!"

I patted her on the head and hurried off to the bathroom. That, I thought, feeling better, is a real friend. When I'd showered and dressed, I came back to the

19

kitchen to find that Molly had cleaned it up. She was standing now, with the dish towel in her hand, staring at the television with an expression of supreme disgust. "What's the matter?" I asked.

She waved the cloth at the screen. "That creep."

On the screen a bunch of cops were hurrying someone in handcuffs through a crowd of jeering people. Whoever it was had a suit jacket draped over his head. "Who?"

"That serial killer. The one who killed all the kids in New Jersey. Buried them in his yard. His trial starts today." Molly shuddered. "He didn't just kill them, you know. He tortured them first. His youngest victim was only eleven."

"I thought he only killed runaways. Do kids run away as young as that?"

"I guess so. Nobody even knows how many there were. Kids disappear every year and are never found." Her face was still creased with disgust. "I wonder how many steps it takes to get from Nick Bruno to that."

"Don't get melodramatic," I said. "Bruno's no psycho. He's just your normal, average bully. There's a big difference between hassling people and killing them."

She turned off the television and hung the dish towel on the rack. "I don't want to think about it. I wish they wouldn't put the story on the news. It probably gives weirdos all over the country ideas. Come on, Muttsy." She leaned down and picked Muttsy up, talking to her while the dog licked her cheek. "At least the guy who hurt you did it by accident."

"And then had the good sense to take her to your father."

20

Molly set Muttsy back on the floor and clipped on the leash. "If Dad hadn't been able to save her, he'd have put her to sleep," she said. "He can't stand to see an animal suffer. What kind of person gets his kicks torturing kids?"

"Like you said. A psycho."

"Psycho pervert creep."

"Let's get going."

"Yeah. And forget about it. I don't want to know there are guys like that in the world."

"There aren't very many," I assured her, as I pulled the door shut behind us. "The world's not like that."

CHAPTER 3

B Y THE TIME we'd parked in the school lot, back next to the drivers' ed cars where Molly always parks when she drives, the sun was out and the day had warmed up considerably. It was the kind of fall day that makes the covers of nature calendars—all reds and golds and deep blue. We walked up through the lot with the juniors and seniors who drive and a couple of faculty members hurrying to the side door to keep Dr. Towson from knowing they were late. The buses were pulling up, one after another in a great caravan, dropping their passengers at the side of the building.

As we turned the corner and started up the walkway toward the flagstone courtyard in front of the school, we saw a crowd of kids standing around the old memorial fountain. They were watching something, but we couldn't tell what. The kids coming up with us and the ones who'd gotten there just before crowded up, asking what was happening and shoving to see. Everybody else was quiet. There was a tension in that quiet that I didn't like. It reminded me of a crowd I'd seen once, gathered around a car accident.

Molly went ahead of me, squeezing past kids, using her elbows when she had to, and I followed. "Quit shoving," somebody said, and the kids in front of Molly squeezed closer together, keeping her from getting any farther.

"Can you see anything?" she asked me, after trying in vain to push on ahead.

Over the people in front of me I could see, all right. There were four people in the open space by the fountain. Gordon Krosky, Matt Singleton and Nick Bruno were facing the fountain with their backs to the crowd. Bran Slocum was backed against the crumbling stone basin, his face unreadable, his bad eye angled so far off to the side that you could see mostly white. His backpack was on the flagstones a few feet away.

"Well?" Molly asked, gouging me in the side with her elbow. "What's going on?"

"Nothing at the moment," I said, hoping nobody would let her through. I had a pretty good idea what she'd do once she found out what was happening and who the target was.

"That hair's greasy," Nick said. "Don't you think so, Matt?"

"That's Bruno, isn't it?" Molly asked.

"G-g-greasy!" Matt repeated.

"We don't like greasy hair, do we, Gordo?"

"Nah." Krosky, a huge guy with a small head and brain to match, glanced over at Nick as if to be sure he'd given the right answer. Nick nodded and Krosky smiled. "Nah, Nick. We hate it!"

Molly was jumping up and down, trying to see.

"It's a shame that such long, gorgeous hair should be allowed to get so"—Nick shuddered broadly and made a sound in the back of his throat as if he were

23

about to be sick— "disgustingly greasy. Let's do him a favor and wash it!"

With that, Nick lunged toward Slocum and grabbed him by the shoulders. Slocum tried to pull away, but Matt caught him from one side and Gordon from the other. They didn't have an easy time holding him, even though there were three of them, and they were all bigger than he was. Slocum flung himself from side to side, cracking Gordon into the fountain with a sound that echoed through the courtyard.

Molly tried once more to push her way forward, and the kids in front pushed back again. Giving up, she turned and began shoving her way back the way we'd come. Kids moved readily out of her way, and then pushed in after her. I stayed where I was, not the least interested in trying to follow her. I felt sorry for Slocum, but I had no intention of having a confrontation with three ticked-off football players.

Nick ripped the rubber band off Slocum's ponytail with a jerk that looked as if it would tear half the hair out, and then they managed to get Slocum, still struggling to get away from them, turned toward the fountain.

"Hold him," Nick said to the other two, as he shoved Slocum's head into the filthy, debris-choked water that was left in the basin from the September rains. Slocum jerked and fought, but Nick pushed with both hands, jamming his face against the bottom, then scooped handfuls of dirty water over Slocum's hair.

There was a commotion in the crowd over to my left, and I saw Molly's short, stocky figure barreling through, using her backpack like a battering ram. She burst into the open and went straight for Nick, bashing him on the back with her pack.

"Let him up, you creeps!" she hollered.

Nick pushed her away, but she came right back, aiming her pack now at Gordon, who let go of Slocum to defend himself. Bran, with only Matt holding him now, jerked loose, muddy water and cigarette butts running down his tangled hair and over his face, and knocked Nick sideways. Nick tripped over his own feet and went down, cursing. Jerry Ritoni came out of the crowd to help Nick up.

Just then the first bell rang, jangling across the courtyard, and the big double doors swung open as Dr. Towson unlocked them. He does this with great ceremony every morning, personally welcoming his students to another day in the hallowed halls of Ridgewood High. Towson, a tall, broad figure in a pin-striped blue suit with a red bow tie, propped the doors open and took up his position in the middle, where he could nod and speak to everyone who went in.

Immediately, the crowd broke up into couples and knots of kids, talking, laughing, jostling each other, heading around the fountain and up the wide front steps as if nothing unusual had been happening.

"Cowards!" Molly yelled, at no one and everyone.

Nick, Matt and Gordon brushed themselves off, patting each other on the back and grinning. As they skirted the fountain, Jerry Ritoni aimed a kick at Slocum's backpack and sent it across the flagstones into the sparse grass.

Slocum just stood, wiping his face with the sleeve of his jeans jacket, while Molly went to retrieve his backpack. Above his head, on the cracked obelisk at

25

the center of the fountain, the brass plaque proclaimed the glory of the ''boys from Ridgewood High who gave their lives in the Great War.''

Kristin, who'd been nearer to the front of the crowd, saw me and came over to where I was standing and letting people move around me. She slipped her arm through mine. ''Those guys don't let up.''

Molly and Bran were walking up toward the stairs, next to each other, but not touching and not talking. Other kids were giving them a wide berth.

I looked down at Kristin, and she grinned, her green eyes crinkling at me. The sun struck highlights of pure gold in her long, blond hair, and I grinned back. ''Molly Pepper's not afraid of anybody,'' she said. ''She'd take on Godzilla. I can't figure out what she sees in that guy, though. Talk about weird!'' She tugged at my arm. ''Come on, Davey, I can't be late for homeroom again or Fergie'll kill me.''

We went around the fountain, heading up toward Dr. Towson, who was nodding and smiling, greeting people by name every so often, and ostentatiously checking his watch every few seconds. ''I've got wheels for tonight,'' I said.

''I knew you'd think of something.'' Kristin did a little double skip, still hanging onto my arm. ''Let's make it a really terrific night.'' She reached up and kissed me on the cheek, her pale, soft hair brushing my face. She smelled fresh and sweet—like a field of wildflowers, and I remembered how I felt the first time we went out. It shouldn't be so hard to get back to the way we were then, I thought. Some time alone ought to do it. By the time we got inside, Molly Pepper and Bran Slocum were the farthest thing from my mind.

Bran was late to homeroom, but he came, a few minutes after the bell, his hair wet but combed and slicked back into a ponytail again, his face clean. The only evidence of what had happened was his jacket, wet half the way from neck to elbows, and a purplish swelling on his upper lip. He handed Mrs. Campbell a late slip and went to his seat, his head up, shoulders straight. I thought he paused for just a second before he sat down, looking at Matt Singleton, but I couldn't be sure.

I had to hand it to him. I'd have gone home. It isn't that I'd have been running away exactly. I'd have gone home to take a shower and change. And then I just wouldn't have come back. I glanced over at him, thinking about the word Molly had used. *Still.* She was right. While Mrs. Campbell finished taking the roll, he just sat there, not moving, quiet, contained and expressionless. He might have glanced at Matt occasionally, but with that eye, there was no way to know for certain.

I didn't see Molly till math class, and then she lit into me. "Why didn't you come up there and help me this morning, you clod, you wimp?"

I started to tell her I'd been hemmed in by people who wouldn't move, but she didn't give me a chance.

"You let me go after those guys all by myself. You and every other person here. Doesn't anybody understand? It would only take a couple of guys *not* letting them get away with stuff like that, and they'd have to stop. God, what cowards people are!"

I just shook my head. "Molly, get real. Bruno is Bruno. Nobody's going to go up against him when he's by himself, let alone when he's surrounded by his goons. Nobody even wants to."

27

Molly slammed her books onto her tablet-arm chair. "Yeah, nobody including you."

Ms. Caitlin started class then, so Molly didn't have a chance to say anything else.

I did a crude sketch of a lion in my math notebook. It was smiling, and out of its smile drooped the leg of an antelope. At least that's what I meant it to be. In a balloon over its head I wrote, "It's a jungle out there."

CHAPTER 4

THAT AFTERNOON I was glad Molly was taking English history instead of Contemporary Issues with me. We were in the middle of a unit on justice in America, and when we got to the room seventh period the bulletin boards were covered with newspaper and magazine clippings about the story that had upset her so much at my house. She'd said she wished they wouldn't put it on the news. From the look of those clippings, she was probably the only person in America who didn't want to know every gruesome detail. Papers don't print what people don't want to read. And plenty had been printed about this case.

Mr. Byrd was standing behind his desk when we came in, and he flapped one long, thin hand at the boards. "Take some time to look at these before we get started. I want everybody to be thoroughly familiar with this story before we begin our discussion."

"Who isn't familiar with it?" Zachary Lewis asked.

"You'd have to have been in a cave for about a year to miss this story."

Mr. Byrd shoved his hands into his jeans pockets and leaned back against the blackboard. "Just look.

And read. There are a lot of viewpoints here. Different perspectives, different tones. *The New York Times*, the *National Enquirer*, *People* magazine, our own *Ridgewood Courier*, *Reader's Digest*. A little bit of everything. And if you don't get enough from the print media, I've got some videotapes we can look at to see what television has to add."

Jennifer Logan groaned. "They must have shown men bringing bodies out of that guy's yard in those plastic bags about a million times. We've seen enough of that!"

Zach Lewis laughed. "Yeah, and cops digging with masks over their noses. I'll bet that was gross duty. You suppose they got paid extra?" Zach could find something funny in almost anything.

Cheryl Heroux squealed. "Do we have to talk about this, Mr. Byrd? It's too disgusting. What's it got to do with justice in America, anyway?"

Mr. Byrd sighed loudly. "Even you, Miss Heroux, ought to be able to figure that out. Joseph Collier's trial begins today. Four counts of murder."

"I heard he killed ten or fifteen kids," Nick Bruno said. "How come only four counts? Why don't they get him for all of them?"

"Eight bodies were found in his yard, but some of them had been there a very long time. Two haven't even been identified. Apparently, the police think they have enough real evidence to convict him on only four, and one of those was found somewhere else. As for how many more he may have killed, we'll probably never know, unless Collier decides to confess. Serial killers are more likely to get away with murder than anyone else, if they dispose of the bodies carefully."

"I guess that doesn't mean in their own backyards," Zach said.

"Don't be too sure. The investigation that led the police to Collier in the first place was about the disappearance of a boy who was not one of the ones in the yard. His body was found in an abandoned gas station. If it hadn't been for that one, the bodies in the yard might never have been found. Now, take ten minutes, and let's get on with our discussion."

For the next ten minutes, we looked at pictures, scanned news articles, read captions. By the time Mr. Byrd waved us to our seats, I was about ready to agree with Molly. I didn't want to know any more.

The tabloid papers were the worst. Somehow a photographer had managed to get close-up shots of the body from the gas station and they'd printed them half a page high in color. The only decent thing they'd done was to show only arms and legs, so you couldn't tell much about the kid that body had been. Arms and legs with cigarette burns and bruises—and a hand missing two fingers. When Cheryl Heroux saw that one, she had to excuse herself and run out. When she got back, she was sort of sickly pale, and I was pretty sure she'd thrown up. Not even Nick teased her when she came back and slipped into her seat. We all felt kind of sick, I guess.

What made it worse was that all of his victims were kids. Lots of them younger than us, some of them our age. I wondered what the guy had said to them to get them to go with him so he could do that to them. In every one of the pictures, Collier was wearing a suit and a tie. He was just this ordinary-looking middle-aged man with a bald spot and glasses. Somebody you wouldn't look at twice. Not my idea of a psycho killer.

Even so, wouldn't they have been able to tell, just looking at him, that he was somebody to run from, not somebody to get into a car with? Or go into a strange house with? Surely they would have seen something in his eyes, heard something in his voice. All the kids, even the youngest, were too old to fall for being offered candy. That's what everybody used to warn us about—taking candy from strangers. This guy couldn't have been handing out gumdrops.

"Okay," Mr. Byrd said, when we were all settled in our seats. "Let's talk justice. Joseph Collier's trial begins today, after three weeks of jury selection. And he's being tried in New Jersey, where the murders took place. Do you think he can get a fair trial there?"

"Wh-wh-who cares?" Matt Singleton said.

Mr. Byrd scratched his beard and glared at Matt. "I imagine Joseph Collier cares. What if he didn't do it?"

At that everyone was talking at once. "Of course he did it." "How'd the bodies get into his yard if he didn't do it?" "The police got him, didn't they?"

Byrd just leaned on the board until the noise subsided. "The first thing you learned about the justice system in America is that a defendant is innocent until *proven* guilty." Scott Handleman groaned. "Mr. Handleman, you have an objection to that?"

Scott's face reddened. "Well—no. I mean, not usually. It's better than the way they do it in Russia or someplace—"

I expected Byrd to pounce, to ask him exactly how they do it in Russia. He liked nothing better than to catch somebody saying something when they didn't really know anything about it. He's good at embarrassing kids, which is why most of the time I just listen in his class instead of talking. But he let it go and waited for Scott to go on.

"It's okay to assume somebody's innocent if he's being tried for shoplifting or something. Robbery, maybe. I don't know—even murder, I guess. But this is different. This is—" Scott faded out.

"Too grotesque a crime for regular justice?" Byrd looked around the room. "Anybody want to disagree with Scott?"

Nobody did. I was tempted to say that there couldn't be different kinds of justice for different kinds of criminals, but I kept remembering those cigarette burns. He'd tied the kids down and made those burns, one after another. And he'd chopped off that boy's fingers—my stomach flip-flopped just thinking about it. What if by presuming this guy innocent and following all the legal technicalities, they somehow ended up having to let him go, so he could do it again? Maybe there was such a thing as a crime that was just too horrible for the normal rules.

"I don't think I understand," Jennifer Logan said. "The cops dug up all those bodies from Collier's own backyard. One of them, the papers said, couldn't have been there more than a month. So how could he be innocent?"

"Somebody else could have buried them there," Mr. Byrd suggested.

I imagined someone sneaking into a stranger's yard and burying a body there while the guy slept. Not once, but eight times, over months and years. Impossible.

"And I suppose the guy never noticed that every

so often he came home and found all his grass dug up and his tomato plants gone,'' Zach said.

"All right, then, what if he buried the bodies, but didn't kill the kids?" Mr. Byrd asked.

This time he was greeted with silence. I hadn't thought of that, and apparently nobody else had either. "Why would he do that?" Jennifer asked.

Mr. Byrd shrugged. "I don't know. Maybe to cover up for the person who really did it? Let's say he had a crazy relative who every so often went off the track and killed somebody. And let's say he didn't want to see this person he cared about go to prison or get the death penalty."

"That would still be a crime," Zach pointed out.

"But not murder. Different crime, different penalty."

"D-d-do you think that's what h-h-happened?" Matt asked.

Mr. Byrd shook his head. "I'm just trying to get you to think about some possibilities. None of us knows what happened, so we can't just assume automatically that things are the way they appear. That's the basis of our whole system. We attempt to look for truth, not appearances." He glanced around at the bulletin boards. "Do you think the man can get a fair trial in New Jersey, or anyplace else for that matter, after all this publicity about the case? Most of those articles take it for granted that Collier's guilty."

"None of those k-kids got a fair trial," Matt said. "Wh-wh-why should he?"

"Okay, okay." Mr. Byrd wasn't usually one to give up, but he must have seen that he wasn't getting anywhere with the idea that Collier could be innocent.

34

Nobody was ready to give him that. "Let's try a different angle. What if he did do it, but is crazy?"

"He'd *have* to be crazy to do it," Jennifer said.

"So you want to equate evil with madness? Does that make Hitler crazy? Pol Pot? Al Capone? Terrorists?"

"It don't matter whether this Collier is crazy or not," Nick said. "I don't care if somebody hears voices or sees Elvis in the grocery. He kills kids, he goes to the electric chair. Simple as that."

On that, there was agreement. Mr. Byrd looked around at all our nodding heads and shook his. "If justice were simple, we wouldn't be doing this unit. That's why I brought all these articles in. A case like this tests our system to its limits. Guarantees that seem right in every other situation are called into question. Just let me tell you this. No matter how awful the crime a person is accused of committing, he has the absolute right in this country to a fair trial. That's what this whole unit is about. Even Joseph Collier has a right to a fair trial. Now, you want to talk about the death penalty?"

"Does New Jersey have the death penalty?" Scott asked.

"Yes. And if Collier's convicted, the prosecution will certainly ask for it."

"*If* he's convicted?" Nick said. "Somebody ought to just lynch the guy right now and make sure!"

Just then the bell rang.

"With that enlightened suggestion, we end," Mr. Byrd said, his eyebrows knit together. "And God bless America!"

CHAPTER 5

B ECAUSE OF THE pep rally that night, after-school practices were canceled. It was one of the few times all semester that when school was out at three-fifteen it was really out and just about everybody went home. I grabbed my books and met Kristin at her locker, Molly's car keys in my pocket. She was gathering her books as other kids opened and shut lockers and pushed past us. As close to her as I was, there was so much noise in the hall I had to practically yell to be heard.

"I'll run you home now and pick you up again about five. Will that give you time to get ready?"

Kristin looked in the mirror on her locker door and ran her hand through her hair. "Look at this! My hair's a disaster." I looked. To me it looked the way it always did—but I knew better than to argue. "I have to wash it, that's all. And press my outfit. It's been squashed in my locker all day. Better make it five-thirty. Where are we going to eat?"

"Peroni's, I thought. Is pizza okay?"

"As long as we don't have to have anchovies. Last time I went there they put anchovies on and I was sick the whole night."

"No anchovies. I promise."

"Anchovies! I should hope not!" Molly's voice boomed from behind me. I turned and found her at my elbow, clutching her books and dodging kids trying to get by on their way out to the buses. "Anchovies are aphrodisiacs. Like oysters. They're nothing but trouble. Sorry to interrupt, but can I have a word with you, Watson?"

"Sure. What's up?"

Kristin went back to collecting her belongings from her locker, and I let Molly pull me out of the traffic into a classroom doorway. "I don't want to dampen the romance of the moment or anything, but would you give me and Bran a ride home?"

I glanced over at Kristin. She was folding her cheerleader outfit and paying no attention to us. She couldn't have heard. "How come?"

"Ritoni was bragging last period about what they're going to do to him after school. Nick and Matt and the rest of those guys are waiting for him at the main gate. If he walks he has to go right past them."

I could imagine how Kristin would feel about being seen with Slocum. But it was Molly's car, after all. "Where is he now?"

"He's talking to Towson about a placement test for Spanish. I told him I'd meet him outside the office."

"I'm ready!" Kristin joined us, her sweater tied by the sleeves over her shoulders, her pink nylon tote bag on her arm. She smiled brightly at Molly.

The contrast between the two of them was startling. Kristin, all blonde and pink and glowing, clothes color coordinated, hair curling softly around her face, and Molly, in her dark sweat shirt and faded jeans, her face

37

pale, her black hair pushed behind her ears. I felt caught, somehow, between them. Molly nudged me. "Ask."

"Kris," I said, "you know that new guy? Slocum?"

"Fruitful Bran?" she said, as casually as if that were his real name. I winced, but Molly managed not to react. "Sure. What about him?"

"He needs a ride. Nick and some of the guys are waiting for him by the main gate. Planning to beat him up. If we give him a ride, they won't get him."

Kristin looked from me to Molly and then back. "You're kidding, right? You want *him* to ride with *us*?"

"Him and Molly, actually," I said.

She frowned. "Isn't there anybody else who could take him?"

Molly shook her head. "He'll ride in the back and stay down. Nobody'll see him."

"You sure?"

"That's the whole point," I said, knowing that Kristin's main problem was that someone might see him with us. Then I thought of a way to clinch it. "You remember that old movie we saw that you liked so much, where the hero smuggled aristocrats out of France? *The Scarlet Pimpernel*, it was called."

Kristin grinned. "Of course I remember. It was so romantic! He kept all those people from getting their heads chopped off. I told you, it was just about my favorite movie ever."

"This'll be just like that. We'll take Slocum out right under their noses."

"Okay," Kristin said. "It'll be like a mission of mercy." She giggled. "It's about time somebody got around Nick Bruno, anyway. He thinks the whole world has to do anything he says."

"You'll be heroes," Molly said. "But we'd better get going or we'll be the only ones left on campus."

She was right. Already the halls were nearly empty. Half the buses would be gone by the time we got outside. Tricking Bruno was one thing. Facing him was something else. "So, what's the plan?" I asked.

"You two go get the car and bring it up by the big doors behind the cafeteria. Bran and I will meet you there." She hurried off down the hall.

"Do you know this guy?" Kristin asked, as we walked down the school's wide front steps.

"Nobody really knows him, except Molly a little bit."

"What the guys did to him this morning was bad." She smiled. "It was funny though, in a way."

"I doubt that Slocum thought it was funny."

"I know," Kristin said, "but don't you think he asked for it sort of? I mean, he *is* weird. You suppose he's a faggot like they say?"

I didn't answer. I just took her elbow and angled her past the fountain toward the parking lot.

"Seems to me," she went on, "that the smart thing to do when you're new to a place is to check it out. You know—you come on the first day in something really plain and ordinary. Jeans and a sweater maybe. And you see how everybody else is dressed. I mean, Davey, why would anybody want to stand out like he does? He'd probably be okay if he got rid of that earring and cut his hair—of course, there's nothing he could do about his eye."

"No."

"But I don't think anybody would beat somebody up just because he had a weird eye."

"Don't be too sure."

39

"Well, maybe Nick would," Kristin conceded. "But not the others. Not Matt, anyway, or Jerry."

"Are you kidding? The others do whatever Nick tells them to. There's the car." I pointed to Molly's Civic, crouched like a silver hedgehog next to the beige drivers' ed sedans. "The glorified roller skate."

"It's cute!" Kristin said. "Except they're going to be pretty crowded in back."

"Yeah, well, Molly's small."

We got in and I started the engine, its putter-roar making me feel terrifically conspicuous. Several kids looked in our direction. Kristin waved to one of the cheerleaders, who was tangled with a guy in a letter jacket, both of them leaning on a beat-up Firebird. "You sure nobody'll see him?" Kristin asked.

"We'll get him inside quick," I assured her. The sun had been shining down on the car all afternoon, and it was hot inside. I rolled down the window and drove around to the back of the cafeteria. I pulled up as close to the doors as I could, got out and leaned the seat forward. Then I stood back and out of the way.

The double doors opened and Molly came out, pulling Slocum behind her. They hurried to the car, and Molly stepped out of the way and practically pushed him in first. "Scooch over and I'll get in this side, too. And keep your head down!"

When they were both in and I could put the seat back, I got in, too. In the rearview mirror I saw Slocum, slouched down, with his knees jammed against his chin. His face, as always, was unreadable. And he hadn't said a word.

"Kristin," Molly said, when she had settled herself so that her knees jabbed into my back through

40

the seat, "this is Bran Slocum, Bran, this is Kristin Matthis. She's a cheerleader."

Kristin turned around, a smile firmly plastered on her face. "I'm very pleased to meet you." Slocum nodded.

"And this is David Watson," Molly went on, "cross-country runner. He runs like a tortoise—you know, slow but steady."

"Thanks a lot!" I started the car again and revved it for a moment. "We met once," I told Bran. "Or at least I sort of ran into you."

"I remember." His voice was low but strong, easily heard over the engine's noise.

"Wagons ho," I said and moved out.

"Head down!" Molly commanded.

Slocum frowned, but ducked his head.

We drove out of the parking lot and turned down the street in front of school. Sure enough, most of the defensive football team was standing around by the front gate. They were roughhousing among themselves, scuffing around in the leaves, pushing and shoving, pretending to throw each other out into the street in front of the cars that were passing—slowly—beneath the flashing yellow lights.

I drove past as fast as the car in front of me would allow. Kristin looked the other way, and I put a hand up to my face. Molly, in her subtle way, turned her head away but stuck a hand out my window and gave them all the finger.

There was a clatter against the back window. "They're throwing stones," Molly said, and turned to look back at them, shaking her fist.

"You're lucky they didn't break the window," I said. "That was dumb."

41

"As long as they didn't see Bran," Molly said. "I can't stand those creeps."

"Larch Street, right?" I asked Slocum, who had sat up, now that we were safely past.

"No. I have to pick up my cousin's kids at day care. On the other side of the cemetery. Birch, just off Broad."

"What do you do—baby-sit?" Kristin asked, incredulously.

"Till she gets off work," Slocum said. "Why?"

"Oh—no reason. You don't seem to be a baby-sitter type, that's all." We drove for a while in what could only be called an uncomfortable silence. Then Kristin turned around. "Can I ask you something?" she said to Bran.

He grunted, and Kristin took that to mean yes. "Where'd you live before you came here?"

There was no answer. Slocum was staring out the window now.

"Bran? Where'd you live before?" Kristin must have thought he hadn't heard her.

Still he looked out the window.

Kristin tried another tack. "Did you go to a big school before?"

"Not very," he said, finally.

"Bigger than Ridgewood or smaller?"

There was a long silence except for the sound of the engine. "Well?" Kristin wasn't getting the message. I reached to turn on the radio, and remembered that Molly's antenna was broken. I began humming.

Finally, Slocum answered. "Bigger."

"I guess things were different there, right? Fashions and like that? I mean, *lots* of guys at your other

42

school probably wore their hair the way you do—and big earrings.''

I stopped humming and fought the impulse to laugh. Kristin, I was pretty sure, hadn't been trying to make a joke.

"A few," Slocum said.

"Well, but it was like a whole style, right?" Kristin's voice was all cheerleader enthusiasm. She had discovered an explanation for the way he looked that she could understand. "The way most of the guys at Ridgewood wear their hair short or else long and moussed—depending on who they hang around with."

There was another silence. I kept expecting Molly to say something, but she didn't. Even over the roar of the engine, I imagined I could hear everybody breathing. I looked in the rearview mirror. Molly had her hand over her mouth and Slocum was studying the floor, avoiding looking at Kristin, who was still turned around in her seat, facing him.

Finally, he answered, his tone intensely serious. "Style," he said, "has always been very important to me."

Molly spluttered and coughed into her hand. Slocum's face was as solemn as ever. I turned and smiled out at the bus that was passing us going the other way. Kristin didn't seem to notice our reactions. She turned and settled back into her seat, satisfied.

Hoping she wouldn't decide to ask him about his eye next, I went back to humming until I turned onto Birch and Slocum pointed over my shoulder. "The center is up there—just past the green house. The white one with the gate on the porch—you can see the sign in the front yard."

"How will we fit them in?" Kristin asked as I

pulled up to the curb across the street from the house he'd pointed to.

"No problem," Molly said. "We'll both get out here and walk the kids home. You guys go on."

Kristin got out and opened her door so Slocum and Molly could scramble out. As they started across the street, the front door of the white house opened and two little blond boys, dressed alike in grubby overalls and T-shirts, tumbled over each other onto the toy-strewn porch, yelling "Bran, Bran, Bran!"

"Oh, twins!" Kristin squealed. "Aren't they adorable?"

Slocum broke into a run, loped up the steps, pulled open the gate, and knelt in front of the boys with his arms wide. They flung themselves against him, the first one nearly choking him with both arms around his neck. The other tried to climb over the first and dislodge him. Molly stopped at the bottom of the steps and just watched, as Kristin and I did, our mouths open.

Bran snatched the boys up, one under each arm, and whirled around with them while they whooped with delight. He was grinning almost as broadly as they were. "How's it going, you little beasts?" I heard him say, before a passing car drowned him out.

"Would you look at that," Kristin said.

"I guess there are at least two people who like him even if he is weird," I said. Three, I thought to myself a moment later, catching the expression on Molly's face as I pulled the car away from the curb.

CHAPTER 6

FROM THE BEGINNING I suspected that the evening wasn't going to do for Kristin and me what I'd hoped. When I got to her house at five-thirty, she wasn't ready, so we were running late by the time we got to Peroni's. Then she mentioned anchovies so often while we were ordering the pizza that the waitress got confused and there were anchovies all over it. There wasn't time to order another pizza, so I picked them off, but Kristin said it still tasted fishy and wouldn't eat anything but the crusts. By the time we got to the pep rally, she was in a lousy mood, and I was having trouble not reminding her it was her own fault.

Things got a little better at the rally. The warm afternoon had turned into a warm night, with a piece of a moon and high, then clouds that streamed over and around it. The cheerleaders did a new routine that ended with a pyramid, and it came off just right. Lots of kids were there, the bonfire was huge, the band sounded better than usual and by the time it was over everybody was full of school spirit, cheering and laughing and waving their blue and gold Ridgewood pennants.

"This is what high school's supposed to be like," Zach Lewis said, as we headed for the game. "Maybe we'll even win tonight. All I need now is a date."

I sat in the bleachers with Zach and Scott Handleman, but I mostly watched Kristin instead of the game. She's the kind of cheerleader any team would want. She throws herself into it because she really cares. She yells her heart out, and when she does her jumps, her short skirt showing off those very nearly perfect legs, I find myself yelling for our team to win, if only to make her happy. Watching her, I was looking forward to the rest of the evening again.

Unfortunately our team lost—twenty-one to thirteen—and Kristin cried. That's how serious she gets. She and Jennifer Logan hugged each other and sobbed on each other's shoulders till you'd have thought somebody on the team had died. I was pretty sure the cross-country team could be shut out at the state meet, and they'd barely notice. I don't know what it is about football.

I had high hopes for the dance, but it turned out to be worse than the game. The seniors had hired a band instead of getting a DJ, and it was a disaster. The lead singer couldn't stay in tune with his own guitar, and there was something wrong with the electrical system. The speakers either squealed or blanked out. Zach said if he were going to find a date at the dance, it would have to be one of the band members since they were the only ones who were willing to hang around. Kristin and I tried dancing, but gave it up and went out into the parking lot with everybody else.

The team had never even gone inside. They just went straight from the locker room to the parking lot, where somebody had a keg of beer and lots of empty soda cans stashed in his car trunk. When Towson and the faculty chaperones came out all they saw were kids sitting and leaning on cars, drinking soda. It was pretty loud out there, with all the car radios turned to a Top 40 station from Syracuse, but as long as the adults didn't take a whiff of those soda cans, they didn't have much to complain about.

I'm not much of a beer drinker. I'll drink one, just to go along with the crowd, but I don't like the taste. Kristin does. She insisted on drinking with the rest of the cheerleaders, who were all clustered around the team while the guys hashed the game over. According to them, we hadn't lost because Hamilton played better, we'd lost because the officials called everything in their favor. It was the same argument I'd heard after every loss all season. Nobody thought to wonder why the officials seemed to like every team in the conference except Ridgewood.

Leaning against one of the cars, watching Kristin giggle with Myra Cunningham and Jerry Ritoni, drinking her third or fourth Pepsi can full of beer, I decided it was time to get out of there. Without the truck, my idea for a cozy little picnic was shot, and a Civic's not the best car in the world for parking. But I had an idea.

I went over to Kristin, who was assuring Jerry that Ridgewood would cream Hamilton next year, and took her free hand. "Let's go. I think I've got a way to save this whole night."

"What's so bad about the night? There's people, and beer—" she looked up at the sky. "And a moon— sort of."

"This is a lousy place to see it, though. I've got

someplace much better in mind. Besides, I thought we wanted to be alone tonight.''

She giggled. "Okay. Let's go be alone and look at the moon." She grabbed a bag of pretzels off the hood of a car. "I'm taking these along, though. I'm starving."

In the car, Kristin leaned her head against my shoulder. "I'm sorry about the anchovies," she said, and took a sip of her beer. "Are you sorry about the anchovies?"

I kissed the top of her head. "Very sorry."

As we drove out of the parking lot Kristin ruffled the short hair on the back of my neck, giving me goosebumps. "So come on, David, where are we going?"

"Someplace secret. A very nice place nobody else knows about so we can be sure we'll be alone. Just us and the moon."

"Sounds good to me." She fed me a pretzel, had one herself, and then finished her beer. "I should have filled this up before we left," she said, and tossed the can out the window.

"Kristin!"

"Oh, don't be such a stick. It's not as if Ridgewood was the Garden of Eden. One little can's not going to ruin it."

I noticed a pair of headlights pulling out of the school parking lot behind us and another pair after that. Apparently we weren't the only ones giving up on the dance.

I turned up Union Street and headed for the abandoned quarry on the hill above town. The quarry is a great place to swim in the summer—deep and cold and forbidden. Parents tell their kids as soon as the

48

kids are old enough to go off on their own that they must never go near the quarry. So, naturally, that's where everybody goes.

There are signs posted around the place that used to say No Swimming. Now the *no*s are spray-painted out and replaced with *good* or *free*. A couple of kids have drowned in the quarry because the sides are steep, and it's hard to climb out if you don't know where the rocks are that you can use as platforms and steps. But even drownings don't keep kids away.

It isn't just for swimming that the quarry's popular, though. The gravel road that goes up the hill and around it widens out on the high side into what's become a kind of parking lot. The view's terrific. Ridgewood spreads out across the valley and up a hill on the other side of the river that runs through downtown. At night from up there you can't see all the crumbling porches or the boarded-up shop windows. You just see the lights twinkling, and the river like a silvery ribbon reflecting them.

"I thought you said we were going someplace secret," Kristin said as we wound our way up through the curves and over the ruts of the gravel road. "The quarry's about as secret as the dance. That's where everybody's going to be."

"Secret I said, and secret I meant. Trust me."

Kristin shrugged, put her head on my shoulder and closed her eyes.

I was taking her to a place Molly and I had found when we were little. It was only a few hundred yards from the road, and even though there were signs other people knew about it, we never saw anybody there. So we called it our secret place. It was a shack perched just back from the rock lip of the quarry, halfway around the rim from the parking area. We figured it had been some kind of office for the company that had abandoned the quarry; it was just big enough to have held a desk or two and some file cabinets. Now its only furniture was a rickety bench. The shack was made of sheet metal that had been shot full of holes by people doing target practice, and the corrugated roof was rusted through in places.

We'd spent a lot of time there when we were kids. The door had been torn off the hinges and thrown over the edge. It had hung up on a ledge about halfway down, stuck against a small tree. Molly and I climbed down there when we were eleven or twelve or so and wedged the door between the wall of the quarry and that tree so that it formed a flat platform for jumping off into the water. It wasn't safe to dive because there were rocks under the water, but those rocks were what made it a great place to swim because you could use them for climbing out again.

Molly and I didn't go there together much anymore, but I still went back sometimes, when I felt like getting off by myself. The view was just as good as the one from the parking lot. The shack was overgrown with morning glory, and the sumac trees around it had gotten so tall that unless you knew it was there, you weren't likely to notice it from anywhere else on the quarry's rim.

There was no place to leave the car next to the path that led there, so now I drove past it and around a curve to where I could pull off the gravel onto grass.

"This is it?" Kristin asked.

"We have to walk there," I explained, and got the flashlight Molly keeps under the driver's seat. "It's not far."

When I shone the light on the overgrown path that led through the tall grass and under the trees, Kristin pulled back. "I'm not going in there. Are you nuts? What if there are snakes?"

"Trust me. There aren't any snakes." At least not at night in October, I thought, remembering the time Molly had found a huge garter snake and tried to scare me with it. Instead, we'd taken it home and she'd kept it in an aquarium until she realized she'd have to feed it live food. She'd brought it right back.

Kristin held onto my arm so tightly she practically cut off the circulation, but she did come with me. It wasn't easy picking my way along the path, slipping on rocks and leaves, with Kristin hanging on me like that, but finally we came out into the clearing and I shone the flashlight on the shack itself.

"Nothing lives in there, does it?" she whispered, her lips against my ear.

"Not so much as a chipmunk."

"We aren't going in there!"

"Not unless you want to. Come on." I led her through the sumacs, the light flashing on the brilliant red of their leaves, around the side of the shack until the view of the water and the lights of Ridgewood opened out in front of us. I clicked off the flashlight. The moon was a silvery glow behind a fast-moving cloud. Kristin caught her breath. "It's beautiful," she said, as a cloud swept past and the moon touched the ripples on the water with silver.

"I told you it was a nice place."

I put my arms around her and was about to kiss her when something moved by the edge of the quarry. A figure stood up, dark against the sky. Kristin screamed and my heart was suddenly pounding in my

51

throat. I clicked the flashlight back on, and shone it on denim jeans and jacket. A pair of hands, white in the light, moved to shield the face behind them. "Get it out of my eyes!" I recognized the voice—Bran Slocum.

My hands were shaking as I lowered the light. "You scared us half to death."

"I could say the same."

I felt Kristin's hand slip into mine. In the darkness, Slocum looked somehow menacing. The eye that angled to the side showed more white than the other and his lip, still swollen from the attack that morning, gave his mouth a kind of sneer.

"How'd you find this place?" I asked.

"Molly told me about it. She said it was a secret. Guess not."

I shone the light on the bullet holes in the shack, then on the litter of faded beer cans and soggy paper scraps around it. "Somebody else knows about it."

"You said it was secret, too," Kristin said. "What'd you come up here for?" she asked Bran. "Is somebody with you?"

Slocum made a sound that was almost a laugh. "Hardly." He looked out over the water. "I just like to get off by myself sometimes. This seemed like a good place."

Kristin tugged at my arm. "Let's go back to the car. You can have it to yourself," she said to him.

"No, you two stay. I was just about to start back anyway. The twins get me up at dawn."

I shook my head. The night was shot, and I didn't have the energy or even the desire to try to save it anymore. All of a sudden I was just tired. "It's a long walk in the dark. You want a lift?" I asked him.

Kristin dug her nails into my arm, but I pretended not to notice.

He stood for a second, as if he wasn't sure I'd meant it. I was almost ready to take back the offer when he nodded. "Sure. Thanks."

Kristin muttered something that I didn't catch. I figured she was mad, but I just wanted to get out of there. I put my arm around her and guided her back around the shack. On the narrow path I led the way, holding Kristin's hand, and Bran followed. When we were nearly to the gravel road, I stopped and Kristin bumped into me. "What?" Slocum asked.

I didn't have to answer. When we stopped moving, they could hear what I'd heard. Voices, and the sound of a car engine idling. "So much for secrecy," I said.

"Hey! Th-there's a l-l-light down that way!" a voice called.

"Matt Singleton," Kristin said.

"Come on!" The sound of feet pounding on gravel came toward us. "Nick! Down here!"

Matt and Jerry Ritoni appeared in the light, and from the sounds behind them, the others were on their way.

Jerry squinted. "Watson? We wondered who was in that car, and where they'd gone."

"Is it Goblin Girl and the faggot?" Nick called.

"Nah!" Jerry yelled.

Behind me, I heard Bran turn around and head back down the path toward the quarry.

"D-d-don't just stand there," Matt said. "C-c-come on out."

CHAPTER 7

B RAN'S MOVEMENTS, SLOW and careful as they were, sounded as loud as gunshots to me, but the guys didn't seem to hear them. Maybe it was a good thing they'd been drinking. He needed to move faster, though. The chance for another go at Bran seemed to be their idea of a great way to end a lousy night. I'd seen what they did to him in the middle of the day on the school grounds. No telling what they'd do to him up here.

Or to me, for that matter. If they found him up here with us, they wouldn't ask any questions about how we happened to be together. Kristin and I stepped out onto the road, and I squeezed her fingers, trying to let her know she shouldn't mention Bran. She squeezed back. I shone my light on the guys clustered there.

"Get it out of our eyes, dork," Nick said, blinding me with a light of his own. "What are you doing up here?"

"Ever hear of the right of privacy?" I asked.

"Where's Goblin Girl?"

"You mean Molly Pepper? I have no idea. Why?"

"We s-s-saw the car and f-figured she was up here

someplace," Matt said. "Flipped us off from that c-c-car this afternoon."

"Nick said she'd have that faggot with her," Jerry said.

"If he's a faggot, what would he be doing up here with her?" I asked.

"Maybe they're both some kind of perverts." Nick blinded me again, then swept the light onto Kristin. She closed her eyes, but didn't say anything. "Matthis, why the hell do you go with this wimp?"

"What do you care?" she said. "You've got Jennifer, haven't you? Or did she dump you tonight?"

"Nobody dumps me," Nick flared. "She's in the car." He waved his light at the path behind us. "Where does that go, Watson? Is there some place back there we should know about?"

"Maybe it's a s-s-secret hideaway," Matt said. "A love n-nest."

I moved so that I was blocking the path more completely. "It's just a path to the quarry," I said as casually as I could. The sound of Bran's movements had faded, but he hadn't had time to get entirely away yet. Maybe he could hide out in the shack. As overgrown as it was, there was a chance they wouldn't see it. "It's nothing."

"Let's check it out," Nick said, and shoved me out of the way. The others followed him, kicking their way through the weeds to keep up with his light.

"You're in for a big disappointment," I yelled after them. So much for the Scarlet Pimpernel, I thought, looking down at Kristin. We listened to them for a moment, then Kristin tugged at my hand.

"Let's get out of here," she said.

There was a shout from Nick and the sound of

someone running. "It's him!" Nick yelled. "The faggot. Come on!"

"Wait up with the light!" Jerry shouted. "We'll break our necks!"

"Let's go," Kristin insisted, and pulled at me.

"I can't," I said, and even as I heard myself saying it, I didn't know why. "Go find Nick's car and wait with Jennifer."

"David Watson, don't you dare leave me alone up here—" she said, and I pulled loose and headed down the path after the others, trying to tell by the racket they were making whether they'd managed to catch Bran yet. If they had, there'd be nothing I could do for him except get myself beaten up, too.

But they hadn't. Nick was cursing as he went, and the others were sticking together, apparently stumbling over each other trying to keep up with Nick and the light. I turned my own light off so they wouldn't see me, and followed as close as I could.

They had come out into the clearing near the shack, and Nick stopped, flashing his light this way and that. The others fanned out around him. "Give it up, faggot," he shouted. "There's no place to go."

"Hey, Nick!" Krosky said. "Look over here."

The light swung toward the shack, and I shook my head. If Bran had managed to get inside they'd have him for sure.

"T-t-trapped like a r-rat," Matt said.

Nick laughed. "Gotcha!" he yelled. He motioned for Jerry and Gordon to go around the shack on one side and he and Matt went around the other. "We're gonna have a little fun." They knocked sumac branches out of the way and stamped their feet as if they were trying to scare their quarry into making a run for it. I watched, holding my breath, as they disappeared around the front of the shack.

And then, as I was trying to think of something—anything—I could do, I saw a movement off to my left at the edge of the clearing. In the pale moonlight I could make out a figure moving as quietly as possible farther in under the trees. He hadn't gone into the shack after all.

The guys would know it was empty in another second or two, though, and they'd be back. There was no way he could get away, or safely enough hidden, in time.

The idea came in a flash, and there wasn't even time to think about it. I took off and ran straight across the clearing and in under the trees on the far side. I stumbled a couple of times in the undergrowth and nearly crashed into a tree that was leaning at an angle between two others, but I kept on, my flashlight off so there'd be nothing to follow except the noise I was making.

I couldn't help grinning when I heard Nick screaming curses behind me. It had worked. They thought I was Slocum. And they were coming after me.

I went on for a few more seconds in the darkness, tripping and dodging the looming darker shapes of the trees, and then put on the flashlight. I had enough of a lead not to worry that they'd catch me easily, and I knew I could be no more than a shape and a light to them. I glanced over my shoulder every now and again, and their light followed, jerking and jolting through the darkness. There were occasional curses as somebody tripped or crashed into somebody else, but still they came. I angled left after a while, to be sure I didn't go back toward the quarry, and the ground began to slope downward under my feet. I was heading for the highway.

It wasn't long before I had to slow down because the light was falling farther and farther behind. Finally, I heard Jerry say that he was quitting. Gordon must have stopped with him. "Krosky, you're a wimp!" Nick shouted. I could tell by his voice that he was tiring, too. The football game and the beer were taking their toll. When Matt and Nick finally stopped, too, Nick's last words were, "We'll get you later, faggot!" I slowed to a walk, hoping Bran would be far away by the time they got back to the shack.

Then I thought about Kristin. She'd be furious— even if Jennifer was waiting in Nick's car like he said, even if Jerry's girlfriend, Myra, was there, too.

They'd probably give Kristin a ride home. The only other choice was to leave her in the car, to wait for me. Either way, though, she was going to be ticked. It looked as if I'd chosen Bran over her. That wasn't it, but I didn't know how I could explain it to her. I wasn't sure I could explain it to myself.

I started back, making my way by the fast-fading flashlight. I was in no hurry. Kristin probably wouldn't have told Nick anything, but I hoped he wouldn't do a lot of thinking about where I'd gone.

When I finally saw the Civic, gleaming faintly in the pale moonlight at the edge of the road, Nick's car was gone and so was Kristin. I hoped that by now she was safely tucked into bed. And that when I called in the morning, she'd understand. The trouble was, I was pretty sure she wouldn't. She thought the Scarlet Pimpernel was romantic, but I doubted that she'd feel the same about being abandoned on the quarry road in the dark.

I pictured her at the game, all sparkle and smile and gorgeous body. It was a great image, and I loved it. The trouble was, I was beginning to think I wanted something more.

On the drive back I kept watching for Bran along the road till I realized that if he was out there, he'd probably be dodging headlights, knowing that Bruno was out there somewhere, too. I decided to drive by his house, just to check. I couldn't go home without knowing for sure that he got away.

Except for a yellow light burning next to the front door, the house he lived in was dark when I pulled up to the curb. I considered ringing the bell, but decided against it. No sense stirring everybody up. Maybe the light had been left on for him. If so, he wasn't home yet. I decided to wait, but I was so tired, I fell asleep with my head against the window. I don't know how long I slept, but when I woke up, nothing had changed. The house was still dark except for that light. I figured I'd done enough. Since Dad wasn't home, I wouldn't have to explain being out so late, but I did have to work the next morning.

I was turning the car around when my headlights showed Slocum stepping over the chain across the cemetery road. He ducked behind the brick gatepost, and I turned off the car and got out. "It's me. Watson. Are you okay?"

He came toward me, moving stiffly. "Yeah. Thanks."

"It's okay. I just wanted to be sure they hadn't found you."

He shook his head. "When they went after you, I climbed down into the quarry."

"In the dark?" I thought of the long drop to the

ledge where the door was. I wouldn't have gone down there for the first time at night.

"There was some moonlight. Molly told me about that platform, so I knew where it was."

I just look at him. "That took a lot of nerve."

Bran smiled an odd smile that was gone almost as soon as it appeared. "Not so much. Got to get some sleep." He stuck out his hand and I took it. His grip was firm and solid. "Thanks."

"No problem," I said.

He started away, then turned back. "I don't fight," he said. "But not because I can't. I just wanted you to know that."

There was an awkward pause, and I nodded.

"Well, thanks again."

"Any time," I said, and he turned away again.

I got into the car and watched till he'd let himself in and turned out the porch light. Then I drove away, thinking that I hadn't meant that at all. Not at all.

CHAPTER 8

"WHY DO YOU keep getting involved with Slocum anyway?" Kristin asked Saturday morning when I called to apologize. "Everybody's going to think you're buddies. Is that what you want? Why don't you just let him handle things on his own?"

"I don't know," I said. And it was true. I didn't. "Maybe because he's outnumbered."

Kristin sighed. "Even if you take his side, he'll still be outnumbered. They'll just beat up both of you. I don't understand the point."

"They didn't beat up either one of us, Kristin. He got away from them, and he wouldn't have if I hadn't gotten them chasing me. Nobody got hurt. It would be nice if we could keep it that way." She didn't say anything, and the silence went on too long. "I guess the guys took you home," I said, finally.

"Thanks to Jennifer. I had to sit on Gordon's lap all the way home. I was *not* thrilled. And my dad was in a snit about how late I was. If I'd waited for you, I'd be grounded."

"Lucky you didn't, then."

"Yeah, lucky."

"I'm sorry," I said. "Really."

"Me too."

I was at the grocery store pricing the week's specials when I realized that I hadn't asked Kristin to go out with me after work that night. And she hadn't mentioned it either. It would be the first Saturday night we weren't together in nearly three months.

"Well, if it isn't the Scarlet Pimpernel!" Molly was leaning out the window of her car when I came out of the store later. "You got plans for the next hour or so?"

"If you call going home to bed plans."

"You can't be tired this early on a gorgeous day like this. I know perfectly well you didn't get up to run this morning and you didn't have to be at work till nine o'clock."

"I had to leave a certain vehicle at a certain person's house first and walk over here," I said. "Besides, as you apparently know, I was out a little later than I expected to be last night."

"I've heard all about it and I'm very impressed. Hop in."

"So what's the plan?" I asked, when she pulled out of the parking lot and headed away from town.

"A small social gathering." That's all Molly would say until she drove through the gates of the state park and pulled up next to the picnic area by the river. "Come join the picnic."

A plastic tablecloth covered one of the picnic tables and a cooler sat at one end. Judging from the paper plates and cups, the half-empty cider jug, potato chip bags and bread crusts, the picnic had been in progress for a while.

62

"Molly's back!" The twins came running up the river bank. They were barefoot, their faces smudged with dirt, their overalls rolled up to their knees. "Come see what Bran and us builded in the water!" The first one to reach Molly started pulling on her hand.

"Hold it. I want you to meet a friend first. David, this is"—she squinted at the one who had hold of her hand—"this is Keith. He's the one with the scratch on his cheek. And that's Kipp. Twins, this is David."

"I'm the oldest one," Keith said, still pulling at Molly.

"Only two minutes," Kipp said, scowling. "Bran says two minutes doesn't hardly count."

"Does so, and I'm bigger."

"Does not—"

Bran, also barefoot, came up the bank. "Stop fighting and say hello like civilized human beings," he said to them. "Then get back here. We've got a leak!"

Keith let go of Molly. "Hi!" He tossed the word over his shoulder as he plunged back down toward the river.

"Hello," Kipp said, and followed his brother.

Molly and I joined Bran and walked down to the river's edge, where the twins were bent over their project, scooping mud from the bank. A stone and stick dam stretched from the bank to a log that lay parallel to the bank and a couple of feet out in the shallow water.

"They wanted to dam the whole river," Molly explained, "but Bran told them it was a bigger project than they could handle in one afternoon."

"I also suggested that Ridgewood wouldn't be real

happy to have its downtown flooded out." Bran went down to help the boys, who were arguing about whether mud was enough to stop the leak.

"You'd better get it fixed and be done," Molly said. "It's getting late and chilly, and your grandma's going to skin you if you come home all wet and get pneumonia."

Kipp wiped his nose with a muddy hand. "She won't skin us," he said. "She'll skin Bran. Won't she, Bran?"

"She'll skin us all. And then your mother'll skin us again afterwards."

Molly and I left them arguing about whether they could be skinned twice and went up to the table. She handed me an apple. "Guaranteed fresh. We went to an orchard this afternoon and picked them ourselves. Aren't the twins great?"

"Yeah. Great." I bit into the apple and glanced around. There were people at several of the other picnic tables. Families, mostly. But a hundred yards farther down was a bunch of kids about our age. They were too far away for me to see whether I knew any of them.

"Don't get paranoid," Molly said. "Nobody's going to see you with us. Or care."

I should have known Molly would guess what I was thinking. "Everybody's going to think you're buddies," Kristin had said.

I'd known Molly long enough to know what she was up to. In spite of her protestations when I'd called Bran her boyfriend, she liked him. A lot. You couldn't miss it. And she couldn't leave it at that. What she wanted was for me to like him, too.

"The boys are cute," I said, hoping the subject

64

change wasn't too obvious. "Their mother's his cousin?"

"Angela, her name is. Angela Ridley. She's staying with her parents—Bran's aunt and uncle—till she can afford a place of her own. The father's not around. I gather he never was. Anyway, Bran's aunt says Bran's practically saved all their lives."

"How so?"

"The twins are crazy about him. You wouldn't know it to watch them with him, but they were holy terrors till he arrived. Nobody could do anything with them. But when he came they latched onto him and won't let go. They'll do anything he tells them to do. If they didn't go to day care, they'd want him to stay home with them every day."

"The way things have been for Bran at school, that wouldn't be such a bad idea."

"Snack break," Bran's voice called from the river bank. A few moments later he appeared, grunting and puffing his way up toward us, like an overburdened donkey. One twin was perched on his shoulders, the other was hanging onto his back. He carried a pair of shoes and socks in each hand and his sneakers hung by their laces from his teeth. "Get these dam engineers some chips," he said.

"Hey, Molly! We're dam engineers," Keith hollered. "Dam, dam, dam engineers."

"Get us chips!" Kipp said.

When Molly found out I wasn't doing anything with Kristin that night, she suggested we take the twins home and then all go to a movie. I told her I was too tired. Before she had a chance to argue or question my motives, Bran declined too. "It was one very long night last night," he said.

"Oh, all right, if both of you are going to fink out on me—" Molly said.

I looked at Bran over Molly's head and thought I detected the ghost of a smile. "Some other time," he said.

"Right," I agreed, gratefully. "Some other time."

CHAPTER 9

MONDAY WAS ANOTHER brilliant fall day, the air crisp but the sun so bright that it was too warm for jackets by lunchtime. Just about everybody who brown-bagged lunch went outside to eat instead of to the cafeteria. Frisbees sailed over the fountain and music blared from a car that had been brought up to the edge of the courtyard.

Zach Lewis and I were leaning on the fountain. He was telling me, between mouthfuls of corn chips, that he'd heard the miniplaza going up across from the grocery store where I worked was going to have a Friendly's and he was going to apply for a job there, when I noticed a guy who looked around thirty or so talking to a group of kids down by the curb. Zach saw that I wasn't listening and stopped talking about ice cream. "What's the matter?"

"That guy over there, talking to those freshmen."

Zach looked over his shoulder. "The one in the tasteful plaid sport coat?"

"Yeah. Who is he?"

Zach shrugged. "Somebody's dad, maybe. How should I know?"

"Too young. Besides, there's something odd about

67

him. Watch him for a minute. He doesn't really look at the people he's talking to. His eyes are moving all the time, like he's watching for somebody. You think he's selling drugs?"

"Right here in the courtyard?"

"Why not? Half the school's outside today." As I said that, the guy moved away from the kids he'd been talking to and headed for one of the groups playing Frisbee. "I think I'll go check him out," I told Zach.

"Are you in the market for what he's selling?" he asked.

"Don't be stupid. I just want to see what's up. Coming with me?"

"No thanks. I stay strictly away from that stuff." He popped another handful of corn chips into his mouth. "Food's all the addiction I can handle."

Whatever he'd said to them, the first group of kids was buzzing excitedly when I reached them. "What did that guy want?" I asked.

A chubby, freckled kid answered eagerly. "You're not gonna believe this. Nobody's gonna believe it."

"What?"

"You know that psycho killer who's in the news all over the place?"

"Collier," another kid prompted.

"Yeah. Joseph Collier. Well, get this! His son is going to this school. He's right here in Ridgewood! Living here."

Two or three kids started talking at once, and I overrode them. "Don't be dumb. Everybody in town would know if that was true. Did that guy tell you that?"

"Sure," the freckled kid said. "And he knows.

68

He's a reporter. From one of those big national newspapers—''

"Like in the grocery store," someone else said.

"—he's looking for him for an interview. The reporter doesn't know his name, because he changed it, but he said the kid would be easy to recognize because he has a bad eye and he'd be new in the last couple weeks—''

The sun was still beating down on the courtyard, but I felt a chill go through me as if a cloud had blotted it out. Bran Slocum. It couldn't be.

"—says he's staying with relatives here till the trial's over. His paper wants to get to him before any other reporters do. He says anybody who helps him find the kid'll get his name in the paper.''

"What'd you tell him?" I asked.

The boy straightened his shoulders importantly. "I told him he's here all right—that weirdo with the earing. But I didn't know his name. He went to find somebody who does. Didn't even take my name, the jerk.''

The kids were all talking again, as excited as if a movie star had come to town. By now the man was deep in conversation with a group of seniors who'd been smoking next to the fountain. He would have Bran's name in no time. Probably had it already. Could it be true? I started up toward the building, my mind running so fast I could hardly keep up with it.

Serial killers didn't have families, did they? They weren't normal people leading normal lives. They were some kind of monsters. I remembered the articles in Mr. Byrd's room. The neighbors said that Collier was so ordinary. An ordinary guy could have a son. But even if he did, how could it be Bran?

I thought of Bran with one twin on his shoulders and one on his back, his shoes dangling from his teeth. Joseph Collier's son? Impossible.

Impossible or not, the story would be all over school by the end of lunch hour. I needed to find Molly. The way she'd reacted to the spot about Collier on the "Today" show, I couldn't imagine how she'd feel when she heard this. Worse, how she'd feel if it turned out to be true. It would just about kill her. I didn't want to be the one to tell her, but I didn't want her to hear it from anybody else, either.

A Frisbee came out of the sun and nearly clipped me as I started up the steps. I tossed it back, and saw that the reporter had gone to still another group of kids, a notebook out now. If it was true, Molly should know it—right away. I ran up the steps, through the front doors and past Towson's office.

"Track's outside, Watson!" he boomed as I tore past. I slowed to a walk till I was around the corner and then ran again, dodging kids coming out of the cafeteria. I pushed through the swinging doors, nearly knocking down a short kid who was coming through the other way. Molly was at her usual table, with Bran, of course. They both looked up as I burst in. I hesitated, then walked reluctantly over to the table.

"What's up?" Molly asked.

Bran smiled. The smile was there and gone again, leaving his face expressionless, the right eye staring past me. I remembered Collier's face from the front page of *Life* magazine on Mr. Byrd's wall. There was no resemblance. Maybe it was all just a practical joke Bruno had thought up. He'd probably paid that guy to pretend to be a reporter and spread the story. That had to be it.

"Well?" Molly said. "You came in here like the devil himself was after you or something. Now all of a sudden, you're paralyzed?"

"I wanted to talk to you," I said, my voice cracking. "Alone."

"That's rude, Watson. Really rude."

Bran stood up. "I was just going," he said.

Molly grabbed his hand and pulled him back down. "No way." She turned to me, her dark eyes narrowed, and pushed her hair behind her ears. "So, what's this secret you don't want my friend to hear?"

"Nothing. I—It's not my secret." I turned to Bran. "Maybe it's yours. There's a reporter outside, looking for you. Asking questions. He says he knows who you are, and he's telling everybody he talks to."

Bran stood up again, pulling away from the hand that Molly put out to stop him. "Thanks." He grabbed his pack off the table and stood for a moment, looking toward the main doors, then he turned and headed for the kitchen. He ducked past one of the workers coming out with a bucket and sponge, and was gone.

"What was that all about?" Molly asked.

I dropped into a chair across the table from her, my stomach churning. The story was true.

"David!"

I looked at Molly and swallowed. She had to know. I swallowed again. I could hear the words over and over in my brain, but couldn't make myself say them. Finally, I looked down at the table, away from Molly's eyes, and got the words out. "Bran is Collier's son."

She stared at me blankly for a moment. Then it

71

connected. The color drained out of her face. "Joseph Collier?"

"The serial killer."

CHAPTER 10

"NO WONDER HE won't talk about himself," Molly said, finally. We'd been sitting there, both of us trying to take in the truth of it as the normal noise and movement of the cafeteria went on around us. "What kind of life do you suppose he's had?"

I just shook my head. I had no way of picturing it. Ordinary, the neighbors had said. What would that be? Molly's father, a vet, was ordinary. Zach's, a pharmacist. Kristin's, a factory foreman. Those were ordinary fathers. A lot of times, over the years, I'd envied that.

Once, in junior high, I'd gone with my father to a craft fair and some of the guys from school had come by the booth. They'd listened while Dad, who still had a full beard then, and wore a buckskin shirt and moccasins, had rambled on to a customer about the mystical importance of knowing one's totem, of tuning in to our spiritual connections with the animal world. And the guys had laughed at him. I'd spent the rest of that day pretending to be interested in a potter at the other end of the tent. Wishing for a father who was ordinary.

In spite of Dad's hippie weirdness, though, our life together wasn't so very different from anybody else's. I wondered what kind of life somebody would have with a father who killed kids, burned them with cigarettes and cut their fingers off and buried the bodies in the backyard. Did they sit down in their kitchens to eat macaroni and cheese and talk about what kind of day they'd had?

"Maybe he never even lived with his father," I said. "His parents could be divorced. Maybe he lives with his mother—"

"Then why isn't he with her now? Why did he come to Ridgewood?" Molly kept pushing at her hair, though it hadn't moved from behind her ears. It was as if her hands were acting on their own. "I thought I was getting to know him, that he was beginning to open up a little. But what did I know? That the Ridleys are his aunt and uncle, Angela's his cousin and he takes care of the twins. That's all. Nothing about him. Nothing at all about him." She rubbed a hand across her face. "I feel like I'm going to be sick."

The bell for sixth period rang, and the cafeteria began emptying. Molly stood up and looked around her at the kids talking, laughing, roughhousing as they carried their trays back and gathered their books. "Every single person in the school's going to know about it by the end of the day."

On my way to my free period after lunch, I had to pass Towson's office. The reporter was there, leaning over the counter, talking to Mrs. O'Neil, the school secretary. I didn't see Dr. Towson. I wondered if they'd tell the guy anything about Bran. Probably that was against the law.

I couldn't concentrate on the Spanish homework I

was supposed to do that period. Too many questions were chasing each other around in my brain. There was no way to answer them, but they wouldn't go away.

If Bran *had* lived with his father during the time his father had been killing kids, burying their bodies in the backyard, wouldn't he have known? No matter how ordinary Collier looked to the neighbors, his son would know better.

If every so often Dad brought somebody into the garage and killed him with a chisel between the eyes, I'd know that, wouldn't I? I'd see it in him somehow, even if I was never there when he did it. Even if he cleaned everything up and got rid of every piece of evidence, I'd know. When he looked at me, I'd know!

And if Bran *knew*, then why hadn't he gone to the police to keep it from happening again? I tried to think if it had been Dad, whether I'd have been able to report what I knew, to send him to jail. Or to die.

I drew a hangman's noose in my notebook, then scribbled it over. My father wasn't Joseph Collier. He caught spiders in his coffee cup and put them outside instead of squashing them. One winter when a mouse nested in the base of one of his favorite totems he wouldn't even set a regular trap. He caught it alive and took it clear up near the quarry so it wouldn't come back. I couldn't compare myself to Bran. My father to his.

Maybe Bran's father tortured him, too. Beat him up. Made him afraid that if he told he'd be buried right along with the others. I shuddered. Bran had grown up in a house with a homicidal maniac. I didn't know what that had been like. I couldn't imagine it. Finally, I just couldn't imagine it.

The news got around fast, all right. Everybody was talking about it as we got to class seventh period. "Did you hear?" Jennifer Logan asked Mr. Byrd.

"If you mean did I hear the rumor that Joseph Collier's son is here in Ridgewood, yes." His voice was tight.

"It's B-B-Bran Slocum," Matt said.

"I *said* he was a pervert," Nick added.

"Sit!" Mr. Byrd said. "And be quiet." He didn't slouch against the blackboard now, waiting, in his usual relaxed way, till we settled down. He stood very straight and very tense, his face stern. "I said, be quiet!"

By the time the bell rang, everyone was seated and nobody was talking. "First of all," he said, "the source of this 'news' would seem to be a reporter from a tabloid newspaper. Not what you might call an unimpeachable source. So in the first place we don't know that Collier's son is here at all.

"From what I understand, the reporter arrived in Ridgewood acting on a tip, without so much as a name to go on. He got Slocum's name from students—students he promised would get their names in his newspaper for helping him. So in the second place, we don't know that Bran Slocum is the person, *if* there is such a person."

"It isn't as if there were lots of new kids with one bad eye," Scott Handleman said. "Who else could it be?"

"I repeat that we don't know for a fact that Collier's son is even here." He gestured toward the clippings on the board. "It's true that Collier has a son. That's mentioned in two of these articles. One merely mentions the son's existence, the other says that the

76

boy went to live with friends when Collier was arrested. That was months and months ago. We don't know that he's left New Jersey, let alone come to Ridgewood.''

I thought of the way Bran had jumped up when I told him a reporter was looking for him. That was enough for me.

''But what if he is here?'' Cheryl Heroux asked. ''What if it *is* Slocum?''

Mr. Byrd spread his hands. ''All right, what if? Keeping in mind that we have no facts to support this claim, what would it mean if it were true?''

''It would mean he should get kicked out,'' Nick said. ''Out of school. Out of town.''

There was a murmur of agreement from some of the other kids.

''For what reason?'' Mr. Byrd asked.

'' 'Cause he's a sick, perverted weirdo.''

''Is that a clinical diagnosis, Mr. Bruno?''

''Because w-w-we don't want n-n-no psycho's k-kid in our school!''

Mr. Byrd nodded. ''Now there's an enlightened reason, Matt. What possible harm could come of Collier's son attending this school?''

''It wouldn't help our image,'' Zach said. ''Can you see the chamber of commerce brochure? 'All the best serial killers send their sons to Ridgewood High.' ''

Mr. Byrd snuffed out the laughter almost before it started. ''I doubt that this will turn out to be a laughing matter if the story's true.''

''What about what you said the other day?'' Cheryl asked. ''About how maybe Collier was innocent and

77

he was just covering up for a crazy relative. Maybe Bran Slocum's the crazy relative."

"What a clever thought, Miss Heroux. Except that since the first killings took place more than a decade ago, Bran Slocum would have had to commit a murder before his sixth birthday."

Cheryl flipped her hair back and looked out the window as everyone laughed. The tension that had been building in the room seemed to ease a little.

"We haven't time to spend the whole period on this issue," Mr. Byrd said. "But I want every one of you to remember that we don't know the truth yet—"

"Suppose it is true," Jennifer interrupted.

"If it is"—Mr. Byrd went on, his voice fairly bouncing off the walls—"if it is, I want you to remember that Collier himself has not yet been found guilty. His son, who may turn out to be just another victim in this case, is almost certain to be guilty only of having been born."

The subject wasn't brought up again, but I was glad to get out of the room when the period was over. The whole atmosphere had made me uncomfortable. More than uncomfortable. As we left class, a few of the kids were grumbling at Mr. Byrd for taking Bran's side.

After school Kristin stopped me as I passed her locker on my way to track practice. "I guess you'll stay away from him now," she said.

"You mean Bran? Why?"

"Come on, David. I suppose you think he didn't know what his father was doing. Some of the kids are saying he probably even had a hand in it."

"That's stupid, Kristin, and you know it. Collier started killing kids more than ten years ago."

She pulled her cheerleading pompoms out of her locker and slammed it shut. "Which means the kid was raised on murder. Think about it."

"I have been thinking about it, and I don't have any answers. But neither does anybody else. Do you know everything *your* father does?" I asked her. "If he cheats on his taxes, do you help him do it?"

Kristin turned on her heel and stomped down the hall. When she was nearly to the door, she turned back. "My father doesn't cheat on his taxes," she yelled. "And he sure doesn't torture children!"

"That's funny," Zach Lewis said, coming up behind me, "I thought all fathers did both of those things."

"Mr. Byrd's right, Zach. This isn't funny."

"It's all in how you look at it, Watson," he said.

During practice we ran speed sprints on the track. I put every ounce of concentration into running and broke my best time twice. After that Coach gave us eight laps and called it a day, but when the other guys left, I kept on. Somehow, running around and around the track I could keep the questions out of my mind.

The sun was angling down toward the tops of the trees, tinting everything a dark orange, when I saw Molly sitting on a bench by the track. The hood of her sweat shirt was up, her shoulders hunched against the wind that had sprung up. When I finished that lap, I went over to her. "You want to walk a couple laps while I cool down?"

She joined me. "I went over to Bran's house when school got out. He wasn't there. So I went down to the diner where his aunt works to tell her about the reporter. I figured they'd better be ready, because he's bound to show up at their house."

"What'd she say?"

"She thanked me. She couldn't get off work early, so she said she'd call her husband and see if he could go home—so Bran wouldn't have to handle it alone. They knew this might happen, so they'd planned what to do—they're just going to stonewall. Refuse to talk about it."

"That won't be too hard for Bran," I said.

We walked awhile, Molly kicking at the cinders of the track with every step. "I suppose you've heard people saying that Bran probably had something to do with the murders."

I shrugged. "A few."

"It isn't true. Couldn't be. He couldn't even have known about it. You've seen him with Kipp and Keith. He's not somebody who could torture kids." She turned to me, her face tense. "I admit I don't know much about him, David, but I know that for sure. For absolutely sure."

I nodded. She was probably right. No matter how strange he was, the idea that he might hurt kids just didn't fit. We walked on around the turn and back toward the bench. I was beginning to feel the chill of my damp sweats. "Do you have the car?"

"Yeah, you want a ride?"

"Sure."

"Good. I don't feel much like being by myself right now."

Halfway to my house, Molly turned left around the cemetery. "I want to go see if Bran's home yet," she explained.

I shifted in my seat, not knowing how to say what I wanted to say. All of a sudden it was very important to me to go straight home, to smell the smell of fresh wood and hear the smack of the hammer against the chisel in Dad's shop. I wanted to go in and see him bent over whatever piece he was working on, his hair drooping into his eyes. I wanted him to ask me how practice went, and whether I was ready for the Olympics.

But I couldn't explain it to Molly. Couldn't even explain it to myself. In a few minutes the house loomed up ahead. Bran was out front, pushing the twins on a homemade go-cart.

Molly stopped the car and got out. "Hi, twins!" she called. "Cart's looking good." Bran gave the cart a final shove and stood up.

"Lookit how fast we go," Keith yelled, turning to look back at Molly.

"Keith! Watch out!" Bran called—too late. The cart angled off the sidewalk and jolted over the curb, throwing both boys onto the street. Bran hurried over and helped them up, checking them over, dusting them off, his hands sure and gentle. "You have to keep your eyes on the road when you're driving," he told them. "It's the first rule."

"I'll remember," Keith said and went to tug at the front of the cart to get it back onto the sidewalk. "Come help me, Kipp," he yelled.

Kipp frowned, his lower lip jutting out. "You made me hurt my knee. You don't steer good."

"Do too!"

"Do not!"

Bran grabbed Kipp around the waist and slung him against one hip, leaning down with the other hand to help Keith with the cart. "You're both getting good. Let's go get a Band-Aid for that knee. And an apple."

Kipp, hanging nearly upside down, grinned. "A big Band-Aid? Do I get a big one?"

"Biggest we got," Bran said.

"Me too!" Keith yelled, holding up his arm. "I scraped my elbow."

"Two big Band-Aids," Bran said, and slung Keith across his other hip, lugging them both, giggling, up the front steps. "Be back in a minute," he called back to Molly and me. "You want apples?"

"Sure!" Molly said, just as I was about to say no.

Molly looked in at me, and I shrugged and got out of the car. Bran didn't seem to be reacting to the fact that his secret was out. He was just the same as ever.

He came back, the two boys frolicking around him, their pants rolled up. They sported Band-Aids on all four knees.

"Serious injuries," Bran said, handing us each an apple.

Molly nodded, her face grave. "That was a near thing, that crash."

Keith grinned, apple juice running over his dimpled chin. "Good thing we wasn't going faster. We coulda been killed dead."

Bran patted him on the head. "How about putting the cart away and resting your wounds awhile. Go see what Grandpa's watching on TV. But don't you go changing channels without asking."

When the boys had gone in, the three of us sat down on the porch step and bit into the apples.

"Has that reporter found you yet?" Molly asked.

"No." Bran glanced up and down the street and now I could see the tension in his face. "That's why I'm outside. Any sign of a stranger, and I'm out of here. I don't feel like talking."

We sat awhile, the chirring of a cricket filling the spaces between us. Bran finished his apple and threw the core in a high arc across the street, where it fell directly into the sewer. A phone rang in the house. It rang again, and then stopped.

"Maybe you should talk about it," Molly said. "Not to a reporter, but to somebody—"

"I've got to be getting home," I said, and stood up. "I need a shower."

"Will you be in school tomorrow?" Molly asked, as they stood up.

"Yep."

I thought about the kids in Mr. Byrd's class. He shouldn't come to school. Not now. The phone rang again.

"We'll see you there, I guess." Molly was still holding her apple core.

Bran took it from her and threw it. It landed short, bounced, and went into the sewer, too.

"Thanks for the apple," Molly said.

"Yeah, thanks," I added.

"See you," he said.

The questions went around and around in my head again as Molly drove me home. As I was about to get out of the car, she touched my arm. "He's going to need a friend," she said. "More than ever."

I nodded. "From the minute you first saw him, he's had one."

I waved good-by and then hurried to the garage, where Dad was working. I slammed the door behind me and leaned on it, filling my lungs with the smell of sawdust and wood shavings.

"So, you ready for the Olympics yet?" Dad asked.

CHAPTER 11

W HEN THE ALARM rang the next morning, it interrupted a weird dream. One of Dad's totem poles had come to life, eagle, wolf, bear, and was coming after me, one on top of the other, the eagle screaming and flapping its huge wings, and the wolf howling. I had run from it, first across an open field, then down a corridor in school, and finally through the cemetery, all the time going more and more slowly, like a wind-up toy running down. Claws and beak and glittering teeth had been closing in when the eagle's scream intensified and became the shriek of my alarm clock. I opened my eyes to the pale gray light that filled my room and jammed the button down, pulling my tangled covers up over my head. I was so exhausted from running in the dream, I decided not to get up.

I must have fallen asleep again, because suddenly my father was standing over my bed dressed for work, with a mug of coffee in his hand, whistling reveille. "Since when do Olympic runners sleep late?" he said. "Up and at 'em. Juice is poured." With that he was gone, and I groaned and sat up.

When I'd pulled on my sweats and plodded into

the kitchen in my sock feet, Dad was mopping egg yolk off his plate with a chunk of bread. The morning paper was open on the table in front of him, and the unmistakable smell of sausage was in the air.

"You had sausage again!" I said, looking under the table for my shoes. "Aren't eggs bad enough? Sausage is terrible for you—fat, cholesterol, nitrites—"

"Next to the fridge," he said, pointing to my shoes. "And lay off. You're the runner, not me." He picked up the section of the paper he'd been reading and waved it at me. "Do you know the kid they're talking about here?"

I got my shoes and sat down across the table from him to put them on. "What kid?"

"They don't give his name. Collier's son. They claim he's living here and going to Ridgewood High. Did you know about this?"

I took the paper he was holding out. The whole top half of the front page was about the Collier case. A picture of Collier was in the middle, an article about the trial was on the left, and an article with the headline "Son Seeks Refuge in Ridgewood" was on the right. "Nobody knew about it till yesterday."

Dad poured himself another cup of coffee. "Biggest story we've had around here since the Vietnam protests. That was the other time the bad world invaded Ridgewood, New York."

I scanned the article as quickly as I could. There wasn't much to it. It said that Joseph Collier's son had come to Ridgewood to stay with relatives for the duration of the trial and maybe longer, depending on the outcome of the case. He was currently enrolled at Ridgewood High School. Most of the article was background on Collier, all of which I'd seen elsewhere, except that Collier's wife had disappeared fifteen years ago, leaving him to raise their one-year-old son by himself.

One of my questions was answered, then. Bran had lived with his father. And it had been just the two of them. I could feel the goosebumps rising along my arms as I thought about it.

At the end of the article there was a sentence I had to go back and read twice. "There is no evidence that Joseph Collier's son had any involvement with any of the alleged murders." No evidence. Worded that way, it seemed to leave the door open. They weren't saying that Bran had nothing to do with his father's crimes, they were saying only that there was no evidence. The police only had enough evidence to take Collier to trial for four of the murders, even though they'd found nine bodies. Nobody doubted that he'd killed those other kids; it's just that there was no evidence.

"So, how well do you know the kid?" Dad asked.

"Not very well. His name's Bran Slocum. Molly sort of befriended him when he came, because he's had trouble with some of the jocks from the beginning. Bruno and his buddies."

"I suppose she's doing her Saint Francis routine." I folded the paper so that Joseph Collier's face wasn't looking up at me and nodded.

"You'd better tell her to be careful." Dad tapped the paper. "There's going to be trouble about this." He stared into his cup for a moment, then looked back at me. "Ridgewood isn't just small, David, it's tight—all wrapped around itself like a cocoon." He swallowed the last of his coffee and put the cup down on his greasy plate. "It's a great place to raise kids.

An all-American town. And it's scared to death. Molly had better keep her distance."

"You know Molly better than that," I said.

Dad stood up. "Molly thinks she can protect him the way she does her animals. You tell her he's no abandoned puppy. He's dangerous."

"He's not!" I thought about Bran carrying the twins inside to put Band-Aids on their knees. "You should meet him. You'd know if you did."

"It doesn't matter. All that matters is who he is." Dad leaned across the table toward me. "Listen to me, David. There are rotten things in the world that you can't fix. No matter how much you hate them, you can't fix them. You and Molly are young enough that you still think you can, but you'll learn. You tell her to stay away from this kid. There's not a thing in the world she can do for him. And she doesn't want to get mixed up with whatever happens."

"What do you mean, 'whatever happens'?"

Dad took his Windbreaker off the back of his chair and slipped it on. "People aren't going to ignore the fact that the son of a serial killer is going to school with their kids." He headed for the door, and then turned back. "Tell Molly what I said."

When Dad had gone, I sat for a minute, staring at the paper, trying to imagine what could happen. I couldn't. And I couldn't imagine telling Molly to stay away from Bran.

I drank the juice Dad had put out for me and went out to run. I followed my usual route, concentrating on filling my lungs with air and emptying them. When I passed the Ridley's house, the blinds were all down, and it looked blank and closed. *No sign of life,* I thought, my concentration slipping. It was an ordinary expression that popped into my head naturally. All of a sudden, it had unpleasant associations. *No sign of life,* I thought again, as I ran through the back gate of the cemetery and up the winding road.

A line from the newspaper article came back to me. Bran's mother had "disappeared" when he was a year old. What did that mean? It didn't say she'd left or divorced Bran's father. Was somebody implying that Joseph Collier might have killed his wife and hidden her body somewhere? The idea was too grim to contemplate. I decided to count my steps as I ran. *One, two, three, four. One, two, three, four.* My time on that run was very bad.

When I turned off the shower later, the phone was ringing. I hurried to answer it, a towel wrapped around my waist.

"Have you seen the paper?" Molly never identified herself on the phone; she just started in.

I ran my hand through my wet hair and dripped on the wood floor. "Yeah. So now the whole town knows."

"I'm going by to pick Bran up. Then we'll come by for you."

"Have you talked to him yet?" I asked, stalling for time, trying to figure out what I wanted to say, what I wanted to do.

"Their line's busy. They probably have the phone off the hook."

"How do you know he's even there? How do you know he's going to school today?"

"He said he would."

"That was before the newspaper article. Maybe

he's changed his mind. Maybe he's on his way to Australia by now. I would be. Or Mars.''

''We'll be there in fifteen minutes.''

''Molly, I just got out of the shower. I'm not dressed and I haven't had breakfast. No way I'll be ready. You go ahead, and I'll see you there.'' There was silence on the other end of the line. I shivered. ''Molly? I've got to get some clothes on. I'll see you at school.''

''We'll be there in fifteen minutes. If you're not ready we'll wait.'' Before I could say anything, she'd hung up.

As I got dressed, I kept going over what Dad had said. It had sounded cowardly somehow. But what could we really do to help Bran? It would be different if my hanging around with him could make things any better for him. But I didn't see how it could. Maybe it made sense to think about how it could hurt me. People already associated Molly with him, but not me. Not yet. Maybe Dad was right.

When the doorbell rang, I had just about decided to say I was sick and just stay home from school. But Molly was alone. ''He wasn't there,'' she said as she came in. ''Nobody was.''

I did my best not to let my relief show, and hoped maybe he'd gone—just left Ridgewood. Then I wouldn't have to think about the whole subject any more. Or face Molly.

On the way to school I half-listened to Molly ranting about the immorality of the newspaper editor. I was remembering the look on Bran's face that first day, when I'd run into him. Like a hunted animal. I understood it now. That's what he was. He'd been tracked down here. If he went someplace else, there'd be someone tracking him again. Whatever his life had been like with his father, it had to have been pretty lousy from the time his father was arrested till now.

Finally, Molly ran down and stopped talking. Her hands were gripping the steering wheel so hard her knuckles were white. She was chewing on her lower lip.

"You can't change his life," I said.

She didn't say anything for a moment. Then, stopped at a red light, she turned to me. "You said last night I was his friend. Well, I am. And don't tell me having a friend doesn't make a difference. It does. I know."

I nodded. We rode the rest of the way to school without talking. There was nothing I could say.

When we turned into the school parking lot, we saw a television news van in the bus drop-off area. Molly parked in her usual place at the very back of the lot, and we walked toward the school. It was still more than half an hour before classes would start, but already the parking lot was filling up and people were heading up toward the courtyard. Not just students and faculty, but other adults. Lots of them.

"I've got a bad feeling about this," Molly muttered, as a woman pushing a stroller cut in front of us onto the sidewalk. An older couple closed in behind.

There was a crowd around the fountain, growing steadily as more and more people came up from the parking lot and down the sidewalk. A few held signs aloft, lettered in Magic Marker. "Kid Killer Out," said one. Another said, "Expel Collier's Son." A cameraman was filming as a woman reporter interviewed the woman with the Kid Killer sign. A cluster of students stood behind her, waving and mugging at the camera.

"Why isn't Towson out here?" Molly asked, shielding her eyes and scanning the steps. The doors, as usual at that hour, were firmly closed.

"How'd this get organized so fast?" I asked.

"It probably started the minute kids got home yesterday and told their parents. I'll bet there were people on the phone half the night."

Molly shoved her way through the crowd around the camera, using her elbows liberally, even against adults. People grumbled, but moved out of her way. When she'd reached the front, she went straight up to the woman who was facing the microphone. "Who are you calling a kid killer?" she asked, her voice drowning out the question the reporter was trying to ask.

"Get off camera, kid!" someone yelled.

"Who are you calling a kid killer?" Molly asked again. "The only kid killer I know about is on trial in New Jersey."

The reporter turned to Molly, and the cameraman switched his angle to get her completely into the picture. "Are you a student here?" the reporter asked.

Molly, her eyes snapping, spoke directly into the microphone. "Yes, I am, which is more than I can say for most of these people. And I asked this woman a question. Who is she calling a kid killer?"

"You know perfectly well who," the woman said. A number of voices behind her yelled in agreement. "Joseph Collier's son. We want him out of our school—out of Ridgewood." There was another roar of agreement. "We don't want him here, polluting our town!"

"Joseph Collier's son is not on trial," Molly shouted in order to be heard over the jeers that were growing louder. "He's never hurt anybody and he has as much right to be at this school as any student here."

"We want him out!" someone shouted, and others joined, until it had grown into a chant. "We want him out! We want him out!"

The cameraman backed away, taking in the whole scene, and the reporter angled off, heading for a man with another sign. I saw the reporter from the national tabloid, his notebook out, talking to a woman at the edge of the crowd. I pushed my way forward till I was next to Molly, who was still trying to argue her point against the wall of sound the chant had become.

"Come on, let's get out of here," I shouted into her ear. "Nobody can even hear you. And anyway, they wouldn't listen."

"Collier's the kid killer, not his son," she yelled once more. Then, reluctantly, she let me pull her away. "Towson had better get out here," she said, when we'd broken out into the open by the steps.

"He'll be out when it's time to open the doors," I assured her.

"He'd better have something to say."

I was right about his timing. The doors stayed firmly closed until the first bell rang, and then they opened as they did every day, and Dr. Towson appeared, as if nothing unusual were happening in the courtyard. He stood for a moment, scanning the crowd, and then Mrs. O'Neil hurried out and handed him a bullhorn.

"The school day begins in five minutes," he said,

and the horn squealed. He adjusted the volume and raised it again. "Students are to come inside immediately. Others, please go back to your homes and let us get on with educating your children."

The chant, which had stopped when he came outside, began again. "We want him out! We want—"

"I've been on the phone with the superintendent and the president of the school board," Towson said, the bullhorn allowing him to be heard over the chanting. "There will be an emergency school board meeting tomorrow evening at City Hall. You are free to bring your concerns to that meeting. In the meantime, please let us conduct our business in peace."

The kids started inside, but the chant continued, a little less insistent now as a few of the protesters began wandering away.

"Free speech," Molly said bitterly, as we headed for the doors. The television reporter had cornered Dr. Towson now, and the cameraman was coming in for a closeup.

CHAPTER 12

Bran wasn't in homeroom, so I was able to keep hoping he'd gone—or at least that he wasn't going to chance coming to school.

Mrs. Campbell had trouble getting people to sit down, let alone shut up. Everybody was talking about the protest and arguing about whether Bran should be allowed to come to Ridgewood High, to live in Ridgewood at all.

Finally, she slammed the classroom door so hard I expected the window to come crashing down on her. "Now that I have your attention," she said, "I want you in your seats and quiet. Since Bran Slocum doesn't seem to be here this morning, all this may be so much wasted breath." She adjusted her glasses. "I fervently hope so," she muttered, as she opened her attendance book.

After the all-school announcements Dr. Towson's voice came over the room speaker, as calm and reasonable as ever through the crackle of the sound system. "This is your principal speaking. In spite of the unusual circumstances of the—ah—demonstration going on outside at this time, students are to carry on as usual. The citizens outside have a right to make their views known, but they do not have a right to disrupt the business of this school. Students who wish to voice their opinions on any subject concerning Ridgewood High School may attend tomorrow evening's special school board meeting along with other citizens. In the meantime, this is a school and no student—I repeat, *no* student—is to be released from class for any reason. Unexcused absences will be treated according to official school policy, of which you are all aware.''

This statement was greeted with boos and hisses. Mrs. Campbell slapped her attendance book against the desk. She was ignored. Some kids said they should have a right to join the protesters if they wanted. Matt suggested that everybody should boycott the school if Bran was allowed to stay. Andy Tuttle said he didn't see what it could hurt to have Bran in school, but several other kids booed him down. Mrs. Campbell made a few more ineffectual stabs at restoring order, but when the bell rang everyone was still talking. I was glad to get out into the hall.

"Hey, Watson!"

I turned and saw Zach Lewis pushing through the crush of kids, trying to catch up with me. I waited for him.

"You know Slocum, don't you?" he asked, falling in beside me as I started moving again.

I shrugged. "I see him around."

"Come on. You're friends with Molly Pepper, and she's with him all the time. She must have talked to you about him. What's he like? You think he's sort of a serial killer in training?" Zach grinned a ghoulish grin.

"How would I know? How would Molly, for that

matter? The guy's only been here a couple of weeks.'' Some part of me wanted to tell Zach that Bran was okay, to say that everybody was crazy trying to hook him up with what his father did. But I didn't.

''I have this really terrific idea. I want to interview him for the school paper. That would be such a scoop they'd just about have to make me editor next year. What do you say? Can Molly get him to talk to me?''

''I don't think Molly can even get him to talk to her,'' I said as I went into my American lit class.

''Ask!'' he called after me.

To my surprise—and everybody else's—Bran showed up for math. He walked into class, looking the same as ever, his shoulders hunched a little more than usual, maybe, his chin pulled in close. He took his seat, dropping his pack heavily on the floor.

A murmur went through the room like a river rising. Bran ignored it. He pulled his math book out of his pack, opened his notebook and then just sat, staring at the page in front of him. Dana Farmer, whose seat was next to his, picked up her books and papers and moved to an empty place at the back of the next row.

Ms. Caitlin cleared her throat about five times before she asked to have homework papers passed forward. The murmur died down. While Ms. Caitlin was gathering the papers, Molly moved to the seat Dana had just left. Bran glanced over at her, then looked back at his math book. He stayed that way through the class, looking up only when Ms. Caitlin put an equation on the board. She went on as if it were a perfectly normal day, but I doubt that anybody learned any math that period.

When the bell rang, the kids, even the ones who'd

been defending Bran's right to be there, were on their feet and moving out into the hall in record time, as if Bran's presence in that confined space had drained all the oxygen out of the air, and they needed to get outside to breathe. Molly took her time getting her stuff together, and I could tell she was going to walk out with Bran, who was waiting, as usual, to be last.

When Molly had first moved to sit next to Bran, I'd almost decided to follow her example, to take a public stand on his side. If she could risk it, why couldn't I? Looking at him there, so quiet, imagining what it must have been like for him to come past that line of protesters, I'd drawn a crusader's sword and shield in my notebook. To heck with what my father thought. But now I scuttled out the door with the others.

"Go back where you came from!" somebody shouted as I hurried away. I glanced back over my shoulder before I turned down toward the gym. The halls were always jammed between classes, bodies practically against bodies so that it was like crossing a busy street even to cut over to your locker. Now there was an empty space moving through the crowd like a bubble, with Molly and Bran in the middle of it. They both had British lit third period, so they were headed to the same classroom. I couldn't have stayed with them anyway, I assured myself, since I had to change for phys. ed.

All morning the atmosphere got more and more tense. The protesters stayed outside, their chant sounding faintly through the windows on the court-yard side of the building. Arguments inside got louder and more heated, until the anti-Bran side took to shouting down anyone who dared to disagree.

When I came out of chemistry, Kristin was leaning against the wall outside, waiting for me the way she used to after her free period. "If you see your friend," she said, "tell him to get out of here while he still can."

For a minute I thought she was just adding her voice to all the others telling him to get out of Ridgewood. But she grabbed my arm and pulled me down so she could talk into my ear. "Nick and the guys're going to get him at lunch." Before I had a chance to answer, she had hurried off. Partway down the hall, she turned back. "Tell him!" she mouthed.

Molly was coming out of class behind me. "What's up?"

"Kristin says to tell Bran to go home—before lunch. Nick—"

"Bran won't go," Molly said. "I already told him to. But he says he ran once—when he left New Jersey—and he doesn't want to run again. He thinks if he does, he'll have to keep on running forever."

"Not forever. Just today."

"Then what? What about tomorrow? And the day after that?"

"Okay then, till the trial's over. If his father's convicted, everybody'll forget about it."

"Sure. Like people forgot about Charlie Manson and Jack the Ripper. He's going to be Collier's son the rest of his life."

I shrugged. "Tell him to hide out during lunch, at least."

When I got to the cafeteria she and Bran weren't there. Nick, Matt, Gordon, Jerry and a couple of senior friends of theirs were. I hoped she'd gotten Bran to listen to her.

Usually the cafeteria is the loudest place in school, but not that day. From the start of lunch period there was a kind of waiting hush, so the clatter of trays and dishes from the kitchen seemed especially loud. Everybody was looking back and forth from the doors to Nick and his gang, lounging casually against the first table. The faculty monitors, Mr. Girard, the Spanish teacher, and Mrs. Spitelli, typing, were standing together at the very back of the room, as far away as possible. They were talking quietly, apparently unaware that anything unusual was going on.

I'd just begun to relax a little when I saw them coming, Bran and Molly, in the center of that same bubble of space. They walked through the doors and stopped, as Nick and the others came to attention. Kids starting in behind them stopped too, and then stepped back.

"Well, if it isn't the killer's kid and his girlfriend," Nick said. The room was so quiet that his voice carried to the far corners. Even the clatter from the kitchen seemed to have stopped. Girard and Spitelli stayed where they were.

"Lay off, Bruno," Molly said. But she didn't try to move.

Bran looked at Nick and not at him, his right eye, as always, off to the side. He hitched his pack higher onto his shoulder.

Nick looked around the cafeteria. "Didn't I tell you about this creep right from the first? All you had to do was look at him. Sick. Like I said. Him and his daddy."

Bran said nothing. Molly looked around the room and saw the teachers at the back. She started forward and Nick stepped closer, looming over her. She

99

stopped, clutching her backpack strap with both hands. Gordon and Jerry came up next to Nick.

"Sick," Nick said again, and moved toward Bran, till they were almost nose to nose. Even then, it was hard to tell whether Bran was looking directly back at him.

That seemed to enrage Nick. He grabbed Bran by the shoulders and shook him. "Look at me, you pervert!"

Molly started to move and Jerry stepped between her and Nick.

"My father says you must have been your daddy's little helper, mopping up the blood—digging graves in the backyard." Nick let go and Bran stumbled backwards. "He says you ought to get out of here and quit polluting our town. We don't want you here. Isn't that right?" Nick looked around again, and a few people nodded, but still everything was very quiet.

Nick gestured with one hand and the rest of his gang closed in around them, forming a tight semicircle, edging Molly away and Bran back out through the doors. The kids behind him moved hurriedly out of the way.

I couldn't tell from where I was whether Bran was moving under his own power or whether they were shoving him along. Molly tried to push her way through to Bran, but she was shoved roughly against the wall. She stayed there for a moment and then began fighting her way against the stream of kids who were heading out after them, back toward Spitelli and Girard.

Nearly everyone joined the crowd leaving the cafeteria. I went too, pulled by a force like a magnet, a force that collected kids all along the way. I still don't

100

know why I went along, why I didn't break away, like Molly, to go find someone to stop it. It wasn't as if I didn't know what was going to happen.

Partly, I expected somebody to come and interrupt the procession any minute. Towson. Or Mr. Byrd. Somebody.

But no one did. Mrs. Campbell started out of the faculty lounge, saw the mob heading toward her and ducked back inside. We went on down the back stairs and outside without encountering any other adults. In a few minutes it seemed that about half the student body was gathered behind the school on the grass between the back of the gym and the track.

Once it started, none of us could have done anything to stop it. It was like a shark feeding frenzy, mindless and out of control. They made a circle around Bran and took turns, hitting, pushing him from one to the other, kicking. Bran did his best to shield himself at first, then he began fighting back, using his fists and his feet. But finally he seemed to give up, like a dog being whipped, and just absorbed it all, bleeding from his nose and mouth. Except for sporadic grunts on impact, he made no sound. The spectators began cheering, like the crowd at a boxing match, except that I heard no voices for Bran.

It was Towson who stopped it, charging through the crowd like a linebacker, grabbing Nick and Gordon by the backs of their shirts and pulling them off balance. "That's enough! Stop this instant!" he shouted, shaking them, his face mottled red, his voice crackling with fury.

Bran, already on his knees on the grass, crumpled to the ground, his head on his fists.

"You're suspended," Towson said, and let go of

Nick and Gordon. He made a gesture that included the guys who'd been beating Bran and Bran as well. "I don't want to see any of you on school grounds the rest of the week. That goes for everyone who threw a punch. I will not tolerate violence!"

"What about the football game Friday?" Nick asked. "What about practice?"

Towson shook his head. "You should have thought of that before you started this. Get going. Now!" He turned to the rest of us. "Go back inside. This is a school, not a Roman circus."

Molly, who had apparently come out behind Towson, hurried through the crowd, her hands full of wet paper towels. She knelt next to Bran and touched him gently on the cheek. That was the last I saw as Towson herded us all inside.

CHAPTER 13

I USUALLY SPEND my free period after lunch in the library. Sometimes I do homework, sometimes I join the group that hangs out at a table near the magazine racks, talking—quietly, so Mrs. Davidson, the librarian, doesn't kick anybody out.

When I went through the swinging doors that day the usual group was already in place, talking excitedly. Mrs. Davidson was reading at her desk, ignoring the noise.

"—nothing compared to what his father did to those kids," Scott Handleman was saying as I started toward the table. "One of the articles I read said they must have screamed a lot. Collier must have gotten off on that."

Jill Brandon shuddered. "That's so gross! Don't talk about it."

"So if they screamed, how could Collier's own kid not know what was going on? He had to, didn't he?"

"Not necessarily," Evan Lawton said.

"All I know is I don't feel sorry for him because of a bloody nose."

I nodded to them, went past the table and pretended to be looking for a book in the stacks. I didn't want any part of the conversation.

"It was a lot more than a bloody nose," I heard Evan say. "And as bad a beating as he was taking, he didn't holler about it. You have to give him that."

Scott snorted. "I don't have to give him anything. He's spooky, that's what he is. And you don't even have to know about his father to see that."

I didn't want to hear any more. When I got to the rear shelves, I slipped past three more stacks and headed back toward the front desk again, still pretending to check the spines of the books I was passing. Molly materialized next to me so suddenly I jumped.

"Come with me," she said. "I'm taking Bran to the hospital."

"Is he hurt that bad?"

"I don't think so. But the nurse checked him out and said he ought to go to the emergency room just to be sure. Bran didn't want to bother his aunt and uncle at work, and Towson didn't want to call an ambulance and have them come screaming up to the front doors. He doesn't want any more public fuss than he's already got, so when I offered to take Bran, he agreed."

"Why do you want me?"

Molly shrugged. "Bruno and his goons are suspended, too. I don't know where they are, and I don't want to take a chance on running into them, just Bran and me."

"I'm not exactly the bodyguard type."

"You're for moral support. Come on, David. Please!"

It wasn't like Molly to beg. But then, she didn't usually have to. Mostly, I did what she wanted. "I've got history next period."

"If anybody'd understand, Byrd would."

I sighed. "Okay. Where's Bran now?"

"At the car. You go on out. I've got to go get our stuff, but I'll be right there."

We went past the desk together. When Mrs. Davidson looked up from her book, Molly smiled. "Dr. Towson asked me to get David for him. He wants him to run an errand." Mrs. Davidson nodded and told the kids by the magazine racks to keep it down. Then she went back to her reading. When we were out in the hall, Molly headed for her locker and I hurried down the stairs and outside.

A few demonstrators, including the woman with the "Kid Killer Out" sign, were still trudging back and forth by the fountain, but they'd given up the chant.

I went around to the parking lot. Bran was slouched in the passenger seat of Molly's car with his eyes closed. He didn't hear me coming till I opened the driver's side door. He jerked and turned toward me with that look—the one I'd seen the first day. This was a person who expected enemies, not friends. "It's just me," I said. "Molly'll be here in a minute."

I climbed into the backseat, where I had to practically fold myself in half to fit. Getting settled, I bumped Bran's seat back and he groaned. "Sorry."

I could hardly believe the condition of his face. I'd seen guys with black eyes before, but this was way beyond that. His bad eye was swollen completely shut, his lips were puffed, purple and badly cut up, and his face was bruised and streaked with dried blood. "You look awful! Are you okay?"

After a moment he answered, his voice coming thickly between his swollen lips. "I'll survive."

"I hope it's okay for me to ride along." He nodded

105

gingerly, and neither of us had anything to say after that. The car was warm and stuffy. "Molly said she'd be here soon. I don't know what's taking her so long."

Bran didn't answer. I stared at the faded knees of my jeans, a few inches from my nose. They'd wear through soon, I thought. The cloth was almost white.

"I didn't know," Bran said, his voice so low I could hardly hear.

"What?"

"I didn't know what my father was doing." I couldn't think of anything to say to that. After a moment he went on. "He didn't bring them to the house. Not till afterwards. Till they were dead." He touched his lips with one hand. His knuckles were scraped raw. "I didn't know then, either. That's the truth."

I just nodded.

"He used to dig in the backyard sometimes. Said we had trouble with the septic tank." Bran rubbed the ear with the gold hoop. There was blood there, too. "I *did* help him dig once. We dug a long time but didn't find the tank. Next morning the hole was filled in. He said we'd been digging in the wrong place, that the tank was closer to the house." He swallowed. Clearly, it hurt him to talk. "He didn't dig closer, though. Said whatever the problem was, it had gone away. I believed him."

"Why shouldn't you? I would have believed that if my dad—" I let the sentence hang there unfinished. My dad wasn't Joseph Collier.

We sat for a while in silence again, and then he went on. "I built a fort in the corner of the yard when I was a kid. They found three of them right there. Right where my fort had been."

I remembered the television pictures of a place with a tall wooden fence in the background, surrounded

106

by cop cars with blinking lights, a rescue van pulled up next to a huge pit, and guys carrying plastic body bags from the pit to the van. It hadn't looked much like a backyard where a kid might build a fort.

The jingle of keys announced Molly's arrival. She opened the door and got in. "David, you keep an eye out for Bruno and the others. And don't tell me I'm paranoid." She eyed Bran critically. "You're looking worse by the minute. I hope the emergency room isn't busy this time of day."

Bran shook his head and then groaned. "I don't need the hospital. Just get me home."

"The nurse said—"

"She said she didn't think anything was broken. She wants me at the hospital to protect the school, that's all. In case I decide to sue somebody."

Molly shook her head. "You ought to get X rays. You can't know for sure—"

"I know."

She still wasn't convinced, but even Molly couldn't force him. "You should at least file a complaint. What they did to you was criminal assault. I could take you to the police. We'll be witnesses." I cleared my throat, to let her know I didn't want her speaking for me, but she didn't take any notice.

"I've had enough police, thanks. Just home."

Molly started the car. "Towson knew who started that fight. I think he suspended you along with the others so you'd have an excuse not to come back for a while."

Bran grunted. "Or so he could get the killer's kid out of his school."

"Towson's okay," she said. "You'll see."

We drove the rest of the way without talking. I was

107

wondering what it must have been like for Bran to find out he'd helped dig one of the graves. Had that been any worse than the rest of it?

"Who's that on your porch?" Molly asked as we neared the house.

"Don't know," Bran said.

I looked between them and recognized the reporter from the tabloid. He was wearing the same jacket. "Don't stop," I told Molly as she started to pull over to the curb behind a red Volkswagen beetle. "That's the reporter who was asking about Bran yesterday. The one who started it all."

Molly started to pull out again, but Bran put his hand on the wheel. "Stay. If he doesn't get me now, he'll just hang around till he does. I'd rather get rid of him before the twins come home."

"You don't have to talk to him," Molly said.

"What I don't say, he'll make up."

"He'll make it up, anyway," I pointed out. "I don't know why he's even bothering to look for you."

We found out soon enough. The moment we started to get out of the car the guy was on his feet, unslinging a camera he was wearing over his shoulder. I hadn't seen the camera. He knew his business with it. I had barely begun untangling myself from the backseat when the clicking started. Molly tried to get around the car and in front of Bran, but at least ten pictures—maybe more—had been taken in the time it took her to get completely between them.

Later, blown up on the front page of the guy's paper, the color picture they used made Bran look as if he'd been hit by a truck. It had been touched up so that the dried blood on his face and shirt was brilliant red. They ran it with a picture of the demonstrators,

108

faces and signs clustered together so that it looked as if there had been hundreds of them. The headline said, "Killer's Son Beaten by Enraged Mob."

Molly shook her fist at the guy. "You've got your pictures, now go back under your rock."

"You got me all wrong, kid," the guy said, snapping the lens cover onto his camera. "I want to help him. I want to tell the world his side of the story."

"You've done a great job of helping already," Molly said. "If it wasn't for you, nobody would know who he is. His blood is on your hands."

The guy just laughed. "Looks to me like it's mostly on his shirt. Doug McKenzie." He held his hand out to Bran, and when Bran didn't take it, dropped it with a little shrug. "I want to talk, Bran, that's all. Just a little talk. You can have your friends with you to be sure I don't bully you or anything."

Bran, limping, pushed past Molly and went around the reporter as if he weren't there. He stumbled on the steps and caught himself against the iron rail, then pulled open the screen and pushed against the door. It opened. "I guess we ought to learn to lock up," he said, and turned back to the reporter. "I'll talk inside. I need ice for my eye." He looked at us. "Come on in."

I thought about missing history class, then went in with the others. Mr. Byrd was the one teacher I was sure would understand. If Bran was going to talk to this jerk, I wanted to be there. That much I could do.

A few minutes later we were all sitting around the table in the Ridleys' kitchen. Bran had washed and put on a clean T-shirt while Molly made him an ice pack. He held the pack to his face now while McKenzie, like an eager ferret, pulled a miniature tape

109

recorder out of an inside pocket and set it on the table. He looked questioningly at Bran before turning it on. Bran nodded. "I'd just like for you to tell your story," McKenzie said.

Bran sat for a moment, staring down at the red Formica table top. Then he looked up. "Which story?"

"You know. Tell me about your father."

Bran moved the ice pack to the other side of his face, groaning a little as it touched. "Not much to tell," he said. "I always thought he was a pretty ordinary father. Of course, he was the only one I had. He did regular father stuff—bought me my first bike. Strapped me for stealing apples from a neighbor's tree. Worked hard. Paid the bills."

I thought of my dad again, a father who didn't always manage to pay the bills.

"Were you aware of what he was doing?"

Bran turned to Molly. "Get some cider, would you? The glasses are over the sink." He didn't say any more until there was a glass of cider in front of each of us. "Did I know his hobby was picking up runaways and murdering them? No. And neither did anybody else. You've talked to the neighbors—" McKenzie nodded. "So you know that everybody thought my father was okay. He always insisted that we mow the grass and paint the house and shovel the sidewalks." Bran lifted his glass and winced as the cider touched his lips. "He had a thing about being a good neighbor. Worked at it. Just like everybody said, he was this nice, plain, normal guy. Except inside his head. And nobody ever saw inside his head. Not the neighbors. Not me."

McKenzie took out a notebook and jotted a couple

110

of notes. I tried to see what he'd written, but from where I was it was only a scrawl. "Do you think your father is crazy?"

"The psychiatrists say he's sane enough for a trial." Bran made a sound in the back of his throat that might have been a laugh. "You want to know something funny? Really funny?"

"Sure."

Bran fingered his earring. "The only real fight I ever had with my father was about this earring, and my hair and the way I dress. He wanted me to look super respectable. Short hair, sweaters, khakis. Mainstream stuff. He used to talk about how important it was not to stand out. I thought he was dull, you know? The blue suits and striped ties and white shirts. Isn't that funny? I thought my father was dull." He shifted the ice pack. A crack at the corner of his mouth had opened up again and was bleeding slightly. The tape recorder hissed on, and I wondered if it was strong enough to pick up the sound of the refrigerator motor coming on that seemed to fill the kitchen.

"I wanted to be different," Bran said. "That's funny, too. I *wanted* to stand out. Be noticed." He looked at the reporter. "Looks like I got my wish."

"Did your father abuse you?" McKenzie asked.

Bran took another sip of his cider, winced again, and set it down. "No. He strapped me a few times, like I said. But that's all. I have all my fingers and toes. And no scars." He pulled at his T-shirt. "You want to see?"

"Not necessary," McKenzie said, and wrote in his notebook.

"My father didn't do *this* to me," Bran said, moving the ice pack again. "Nice, respectable small-town boys did this."

111

"Why do you think they did that to you?"

Bran shrugged.

McKenzie sighed. "What did you think about the demonstration at the school today?"

"I loved it, what do you think?"

"It doesn't help to play games with me."

Bran snorted. "What does help?"

"Are you going back to school tomorrow?"

"I thought you were such a hot-spot reporter," Molly broke in. "How come you don't know he was suspended?"

"For fighting. I could have hurt those guys real bad," Bran said.

"Then you won't have to go past the protesters again," McKenzie said, and drained his cider glass. He started to put his notebook away and I thought the interview was over. But then he leaned toward Bran. "Do you remember your mother?"

Bran didn't answer. I glanced at my watch. History would be nearly over. The reporter opened his mouth, as if to ask the question again, just as Bran spoke.

"All I know about my mother is her name, Caroline Slocum Collier." He paused for a moment. "That's not true. I also know that she's dead."

McKenzie jotted something in his notebook. "Do you know how she died?"

"Car accident. She was hit by a drunk driver, six months after she left my father. My aunt was with her at the hospital when she died. Sorry if that's a disappointment, but my father didn't kill her and bury her in the basement. Or cut her up and feed her to me for dinner. The truth doesn't make the kind of exciting story your paper likes. Maybe you could stick an alien in somewhere to spice it up."

112

"With your father," McKenzie said, "we don't need any alien."

Molly smacked her cider glass down on the table and Bran shook his head at her.

McKenzie did put his notebook away then. "Just one more question."

"Shoot."

"You ever hear of a movie called *The Bad Seed*?"

"No," Bran said.

"It's about a very sweet-looking little girl who kills people. Nobody wants to believe it at first. Turns out she's adopted. Turns out her real mother was a homicidal maniac. Bad seed, get it?"

Bran didn't say anything. He just sat there, looking at the reporter.

Molly leaned over the table and switched off the tape recorder. "I think that's about enough." She stood up and when she spoke to McKenzie her voice was venomous. "Don't you think you should be getting back to New Jersey in case something's happening with the *real* story?"

Bran started to get up, and Molly waved him down. "David'll show him out, won't you, David?"

I pushed myself away from the table and stood as McKenzie slipped his recorder back into his inside pocket.

Bran continued to stare at him. "Bad seed," he said, finally. "If that's what I am, I'm a late bloomer. I haven't killed a single person yet. Maybe I'll let you know when I'm ready to start. You can be a witness. Bring your camera. You'd like the blood."

I started out of the kitchen, McKenzie following. He turned back in the doorway. "I'm not your enemy," he said to Bran. "Your father is. He became

113

that the first time he turned a kid as alive as the three of you into a bloody corpse.''

"I'm glad you told me that," Bran said. "I might have missed it otherwise.''

CHAPTER 14

AFTER THE REPORTER left, Molly offered to pick the twins up at day care so Bran could go to bed. He nodded gratefully, started to get up, groaned, and sat back down. I realized, suddenly, how much pain he was fighting, and went to help him up. He'd held himself together so well for the reporter that in spite of how terrible he looked, his face all swollen and discolored, I'd almost forgotten the battering he'd taken.

As I watched him drag himself up the stairs, hanging onto the rail with both hands, I wondered which pain was harder to handle, the outside pain of the cuts and bruises, or the inside pain that must have taken over his life the day he found out about his father. He was sixteen. The same age as me. Just watching him I felt like a little kid. I wished I could go home, crawl into bed and pull the covers up over me while the grownups fixed whatever was wrong with the world. I knew, but I hated knowing, that they couldn't do it.

Molly and I went to pick up Kipp and Keith. They had twin fits that Bran wasn't with us. Molly explained that he was very, very tired and was home taking a nap, but the boys said he was too old for naps. Once we got them home, we had to keep them outside, pushing them up and down the block on their go-cart, to keep them from charging upstairs to rout Bran out to play with them.

We were still there when Bran's uncle got home. When he asked where Bran was, and Kipp started in again about how Bran was too old for taking naps, I went inside with Mr. Ridley to explain what had happened. Mr. Ridley was older than Dad, probably in his fifties, but in spite of his sparse hair and paunch, he looked strong—tough. He didn't look like someone I'd want to cross.

As he listened, he closed his eyes and I could see a muscle begin to twitch along his jaw. When I'd finished, he brought one fist down on the back of a chair so hard I jumped. "I'm calling the cops," he said. "We'll give those kids something to think about."

"Excuse me," I said, "but we suggested that already, and Bran says he's had enough of police."

Mr. Ridley shook his head. "Well, he's not me. If we don't get the cops into this now, those punks'll be after him again, as bad and maybe worse. If you don't fight back they run all over you." When I went back outside, he was dialing the phone.

When Angela, the twins' mother, got home from work, Molly and I left. Molly frowned into the growing dark as she drove, her mouth a tight line. I wondered what she was thinking about. As I started to get out at my house, she spoke for the first time. "Do you think there's any such thing as a 'bad seed'?"

I thought about it for a minute, then shook my head. "That's just some Hollywood invention. I don't believe murder's genetic."

"I don't either." She shifted into reverse. "I don't know what Bran thinks, though."

I waved and stood watching as she backed out of our drive. Did Bran believe it? Had that been part of the pain he'd been fighting as he went up those stairs? I shook the thought away.

As usual, Dad was in his workshop. The house was dark, but light poured out of the window in the garage door, cutting through the gray dusk. If a kid could inherit that kind of thing from a parent, wouldn't I go my own way, like Dad, doing my own thing, no matter how weird it was, and thumbing my nose at the rest of the world? And wouldn't my thing be totems? Wouldn't I be in the garage with Dad right now, gouging away at a hunk of wood with a carving knife or banging away with a chisel?

I tried to imagine it. Watson and Son, Carvers Extraordinaires, Makers of Personal and Garden Totems. No way. I pushed the door open and stuck my head inside. "Is supper on yet?"

Dad looked up from the piece he was working on, and wiped his smudged face with one sleeve. He grinned. "Almost. I thawed some chicken."

"I'm impressed," I said, and noticed for the first time in my life how much the dark blue eyes looking at me from my father's face were like the eyes that looked at me from the mirror every morning. The graying hair, the shaggy mustache, the cheekbones, those were different. The eyes were the same.

The next morning there were pictures of the protest on the front page of the paper, along with an interview with a couple of the sign carriers and a short article about the emergency school board meeting that night. Dad read it, shaking his head and grumbling about the small-minded meanness of the citizens of Ridgewood. He reminded me to warn Molly not to get involved. "You can't win against the haters," he said. "There's no sense trying. The only safe thing is to avoid confrontations and hope they leave you alone." I hadn't told him about the beating, or that we'd taken Bran home afterwards. I decided not to.

As I walked to school, I was afraid that things would be even worse than the day before, but when I got there only a few diehard pickets were circling the fountain. Then I saw that there were four new ones clustered at the bottom of the steps, staying well away from the others. One of them carried a sign that said "Land of the Free." Another's said "Public School for All."

"The great placard battle," Zach Lewis said as we went into English class. "Pretty disappointing turn-out for both sides, I'd say. Ridgewood can't seem to muster up a really good fight."

"Which side are you on?" I asked him.

"Who, me? Take sides? I'm a floater, Watson, you know that. Just like you. The minute you take sides you got enemies. I just keep my head down and try to preserve my pudgy self."

The atmosphere at school wasn't bad. Without Bran there for a target or Nick and the guys to keep everybody stirred up, things were almost normal. I stayed out of the conversations about Bran I encountered and did a fair job of convincing myself that Zach was right. Ridgewood wouldn't, or couldn't, muster a major battle over this, and it would eventually blow over. People would get tired of it. Everything would go back to the way it had been before. After all, I told myself, it was only a few people who were upset in the first place.

We had a regional track meet coming up in two weeks, so Coach Morelli worked us hard at practice, giving me an extra hill run because I'd missed practice the day before. I didn't mind. By the time we got back to shower and change, I was so tired that I wasn't thinking about anything except a decent meal and bed. But halfway through supper, Molly called. "Pick you up at quarter of," she said.

"What for?"

"What for? The school board meeting, of course."

"No way. I'm doing my math and hitting the sack. I'm wiped."

"David, we *have* to go. The crazies are trying to have Bran kicked out. We can't let that happen."

"We can't do anything about it," I protested, knowing already that it was no use arguing. Knowing that I would go. It wasn't just that I could never stand against Molly. I'd sat in the Ridleys' kitchen and listened to Bran talk, watched him fighting a pain I couldn't even imagine. Somehow, I'd become a part of it.

Zach Lewis had been wrong. By the time Molly and I squeezed into the back of the room where they were holding the meeting, it was obvious that Ridgewood could muster not only a real fight, but a big one. We were fifteen minutes early, but already the meeting had had to be moved twice to a bigger room. When we got there only one row of seats was empty. By the time the meeting started the room was jammed with people sitting in the aisles and standing three deep against the walls.

119

At a long table on a raised platform in front sat Dr. Towson; Dr. Lyons, the superintendent; and a bunch of people who must have been school board members. Off to the side but on the platform with them sat Mayor Mahoney. "I don't know what he's doing here," Molly whispered. "I don't think he's got anything to say about what the school board does."

"He's probably just here to be sure everybody sees him. He's up for election next year."

When the meeting started, Mr. Sullivan, the president of the board, said they'd begin with the public part of the meeting, and when they'd heard people out, they'd go into executive session. He had to pound his gavel a few times to get order after that announcement. Two different television stations were there, with cameras and lights, and they were told they were welcome to stay until the public part of the meeting was over.

Microphones had been set up, one on each side of the room, and people were to make their statements into those. "Please keep your remarks brief," Sullivan said, glancing at the watch he'd laid on the table in front of him. "We would all like to get home at a reasonable hour. As you know, the subject of this meeting is the presence at Ridgewood High School of the son of Joseph Collier, the man currently on trial in New Jersey for the torture slayings of four children.

"I'm sure you're all aware that there are laws governing the eligibility of New York citizens for public education. We cannot change those laws here tonight. We can only decide what is the best way to handle our obligations within them. Before we invite statements from the floor, Dr. John Towson, principal of Ridgewood High, will explain the legal situation."

Towson explained that Bran's aunt, a longtime resident of Ridgewood, had been granted temporary guardianship, so the fundamental legal responsibility was clear. Ridgewood High School had an obligation to educate Bran Slocum. It was not possible to expel Bran solely because his father had been accused of a crime, no matter how terrible, nor because people did not trust Bran himself. "The boy has committed no crime."

There were only two alternatives to allowing Bran to continue to attend Ridgewood High, Towson explained. One was to request that another school district accept him as a student, and the other was to provide him with tutors who would educate him at home.

When Towson had finished, the meeting was opened to public comment. I could hardly believe what happened then. The first man to speak hadn't said more than ten words before he was shouting into the microphone, accusing Bran of helping his father commit the murders. By the time he quit, Molly had hold of my hand and was digging her nails into me.

Mr. Sullivan reminded everyone that police in New Jersey had never arrested Bran, had never even suggested that he might have been involved in his father's alleged crimes. A second man, with a little more control than the first, said his kids shouldn't have to associate with Bran and that he didn't pay taxes so that the children of out-of-state maniacs could be educated for free.

"Just the children of New York maniacs," I whispered to Molly. She smiled in spite of herself. But joking didn't make the feeling in the room—like static electricity—any less noticeable. Or any less scary.

Then a woman got up and said that our good, honest, innocent kids would be tainted by associating with Joseph Collier's son. That he'd brought the evil and violence of the outside world to our town. "This has always been a safe place to raise kids and we want to keep it that way," she said. A lot of people shouted out their agreement with her, as they had with the man before her. Mr. Sullivan was having to pound his gavel a lot to keep order.

Molly had just told me she was going to get up and say that Bran was a lot less violent than the "good, honest, innocent" Ridgewood kids who'd beaten him bloody, when Mr. Byrd went up to the microphone.

When he began to speak, the audience got quiet so they could hear. "I don't personally know the student in question," he began, "but I'd like to remind everyone here that none of you know this boy either. How do you think he will harm your sons or daughters? As I'm sure you know, the boy was badly beaten on the school grounds yesterday, so it would appear that the harm has gone the other way."

"He got what he deserved!" a woman's voice called out.

"How do you know what he deserved?" Mr. Byrd asked, his voice rising. "What his father may or may not have done has absolutely nothing to do with the boy. Neither does it in any way change his absolute right to receive an education, the same right your own children have, I would remind you."

"Sit down, Byrd," someone shouted from behind me. I turned and saw that it was Nick Bruno's father. "We all know where you stand."

"Yeah, pinko jerk!"

"We know the kind of commie propaganda you been teaching our kids."

"If you deny a person's rights because you don't like him," Mr. Byrd shouted into the mike, "or because you don't like his father, who do you think is going to guarantee *your* rights against someone who doesn't like you—or *your* father?"

Mr. Byrd went on speaking, but even though he was still at the microphone, he was drowned out by the crowd. It was hard to pick out particular words in the noise, but the hostility was absolutely clear. I felt I could reach out and touch it.

The gavel banged and banged, but it wasn't until the policemen who'd been standing at the doorway came to the front of the room that order was restored. Mr. Sullivan called on the man who was standing at the other microphone, and Mr. Byrd, his face white behind his beard, left the room.

I was thinking that even with police in the room, it might not be safe for Mr. Byrd to stay, and didn't hear what the next speaker was saying till Molly elbowed me. "That's what that reporter—McKenzie —was talking about. 'Bad seed.' "

The man at the microphone was gray haired and distinguished looking in a three-piece suit. He was talking about a teenage boy who had suddenly, without warning, turned on the middle-class family that had adopted him at birth and raised him. Using a hatchet and a butcher knife, he had murdered them all. During the investigation, police had discovered that the boy had been conceived during a rape, that his father was a psychopath and that he'd inherited his father's violent tendencies.

"This is only one case. There are many, many

more. We know now that alcoholism can be passed genetically from one generation to the next. We are learning that some kinds of mental illness may also be inherited.''

By the time that man had finished, the room was in chaos. One man grabbed the other microphone and said that Bran shouldn't even be allowed to live in Ridgewood. A woman yelled that she wouldn't send her kids to school if Bran was allowed to come back. Other people shouted their agreement, and finally Mayor Mahoney stood up and called to the police to empty the room. Mr. Sullivan, banging away with the gavel, yelled that the public part of the meeting was adjourned.

I grabbed Molly's arm and pulled her out through the crowd of furious people. She was shaking. So was I. I knew nobody could know which side Molly and I were on, but if anybody so much as looked at me, I felt as if it were tattooed on my forehead. ''Good thing you didn't get up there,'' I said in her ear.

She just nodded. Behind us, a man said loudly that if Bran Slocum returned to Ridgewood High School, no one could guarantee his safety. I felt my stomach turn over. This wasn't Nick Bruno. This was an adult. A supposedly rational, civilized adult.

CHAPTER 15

THE NEXT MORNING, as I was pulling on my sweats, Dad called me into the kitchen. "Ridgewood's made the national news," he said, waving the newspaper at the TV screen. "And they're doing a feature sometime this half hour. Skip your run this morning. I've already called Paul and told him I'd be late. It isn't every day we make the networks."

While we waited for the segment about Ridgewood, I read the front-page article about the school board meeting. It didn't say what the board had decided, since that part of the meeting had been closed, but it went into gory detail about the meeting itself. Whoever had written it was good. By the time I'd finished reading there were goosebumps all along my arms. It brought back that awful feeling that everyone in the room was an enemy. "It was scary there last night," I told Dad.

He scraped the last of his egg yolk off the plate with his toast and nodded. "Now you see why I wanted you to warn Molly. I've seen this kind of thing before, and you don't want to be on the wrong side of it. After what Dan Byrd did last night, I wouldn't be surprised if a lot of people started demanding that

Towson fire him. He was right in the middle of it the last time, and a lot of people haven't trusted him since.'' Dad shook his head. ''I was surprised when he came back here after college.''

''What did he do?''

''Burned his draft card at our graduation. Two other guys did, too. Ridgewood went nuts.''

''All he said last night was that Bran had the same rights as their kids.''

''That wouldn't cut any ice around here. If the Bill of Rights went up for a referendum tomorrow, it'd be defeated by a landslide.''

''After last night, I believe it.''

''He should have known better. You can survive in hostile territory, David, so long as you don't confront the natives head on.''

''Maybe he thought he had to. What they're doing to Bran—''

''Shush, now, we're on.''

''During our news segment a moment ago, you saw a clip from a school board meeting in Ridgewood, New York,'' the anchorwoman was saying. ''Ridgewood is the town where the son of accused serial killer Joseph Collier is trying to attend high school over the strenuous objections of the citizens.'' She was replaced on the screen by pictures of the man in the three-piece suit, speaking into the microphone last night, as people leaped to their feet around him. Her voice went on over the pictures. ''Last night a psychologist told townspeople that Collier may have passed his violence genetically to his son. Is this possible? Is there really such a thing as a 'bad seed'? We've brought in some experts to help us find out.''

She introduced two psychiatrists. In the next few

126

minutes one said there was absolutely no evidence for the existence of directly inherited criminal tendencies and the other said that genetically determined psychosis was documented fact. The reporter asked if the two were talking about exactly the same thing, and they argued back and forth about that. By the time they broke for a commercial, nothing was clear except that nobody knew anything for sure. Afterwards, the male anchor said that everyone should remember that Joseph Collier hadn't been convicted yet, so no one should assume his guilt, let alone speculate on his son's mental health.

"So why'd you air the segment, you hypocrite?" Dad said to the TV screen.

"What do you suppose the school board decided?" I asked him.

Dad shrugged. "You can be sure what they want to do is transfer him to another district. But who's going to take him? There's no good answer for them or for the kid." He pushed back his chair. "It's what's known as a dilemma, Davey. Give me wood carving any day. Problems, sure—dilemmas, never."

When he'd left, I turned off the TV set and stacked the dishes. Maybe that was the real lure of Dad's totems, I thought. They didn't make any demands.

At school the pickets were back in force, their numbers probably more than tripled, and new signs said Bad Seed Out. A police squad car was pulled up near the fountain, probably to protect the couple of pro-Bran pickets who had dared to show up. The chanting seemed to be directed entirely at them, and went on all morning, so loud, now, that it invaded every classroom. In spite of the police, by lunchtime

127

the pro-Bran forces had disappeared, giving the whole show to the other side.

Most teachers did their best to carry on as usual, but the entire day seemed to be about Bran. Should he be allowed to come back? Was he a walking time bomb, a deadly force programmed to go off any minute?

Rumors sprang up like mushrooms. In class, between classes, at lunch, I heard them everywhere. The Ridleys, afraid for their lives, were going to commit Bran to a mental hospital. Collier's neighbors had insisted that Bran move because they were afraid to keep him in their town. New Jersey police had forced Collier to sign over parental rights so New Jersey wouldn't be stuck taking care of Bran. It was all I could do to keep my mouth shut. The worst I heard was that Bran's mother had left because he'd started throwing butcher knives at her as soon as he could walk. There were variations to that one—some said he'd used his father's gun.

Molly hardly looked at me or anyone else all day. She seemed shut inside herself, as if she'd put a wall up against everybody, against the world. But no wall could keep out the sound of the chanting from outside, or the talk that swirled through the halls.

Zach Lewis had quit floating. "Keep him out," he said. "Why take chances?"

"He hasn't done anything wrong," I said.

"Not that we know of. And not yet. Like I said, why take chances?"

"You don't take sides till you're sure which is safe, huh?" I asked him.

"So when do *you* take sides, David?" he asked. I just walked away.

Coach Morelli dismissed us early, partly because it had started to rain—one of those on-again, off-again, blustery October rains that make you feel cold clear to the bone—and partly, I think, because he was as distracted as everybody else.

When I started home afterwards, my hands in my jacket pockets, I found myself heading for the Ridleys' house. I hadn't consciously planned to go there, but when I realized what I was doing, I knew that all day I'd been wondering if Bran was all right, if he'd seen the television show or read the paper.

I saw the huge red letters before I was close enough to see that Bran and his uncle were on the front porch, with rags and paint thinner, trying to rub them out. Someone had written BAD SEED with red spray paint on the side and across the front of the house.

"They did this in broad daylight," Mr. Ridley said as I started up the porch steps. His face was nearly as red as the paint, and he waved his rag at me as he spoke. "Do you believe that?"

I nodded. By now I was ready to believe almost anything.

"The police came to look. Said if we didn't have witnesses or evidence on who did it, there was nothing they could do. Said it was too bad. *Too bad!*" He attacked the aluminum siding as if he were trying to wipe out whoever had done it instead of just the paint.

"I must have been back in the kitchen," Bran said. "Didn't hear a thing." The swelling in his face had gone down some, but the bruises had turned a darker purple. He still looked awful.

"I hope you've started locking your doors," I said.

"Doors, windows, garage," Mr. Ridley assured me. "Not that it'll keep them from doing anything

129

they want outside. The cops won't do nothing but drive by once in a while to check on things. What the hell do we pay taxes for, I want to know. I tried to file charges against that Bruno kid yesterday and they told me Bran had to do it himself. And if he did, he'd need a doctor's report describing his injuries. So that when the bruises went away there'd be evidence of assault.''

''I didn't want to file charges,'' Bran said.

Mr. Ridley turned away from Bran and attacked the siding again. ''Right, and even if you did, we don't have no doctor's report. You didn't want to go to the hospital, either. So there's nothing we can do. You got to hide out in the house all day and those punks are out roaming the streets with their paint cans, free as birds.'' He smacked his left hand against the siding. ''And the cops can't touch 'em.''

Bran stopped rubbing at the paint. ''Getting the police into it would have made it worse. And they'd still be out here.''

''Maybe.''

''Can I help with that?'' I asked.

Mr. Ridley looked from the rag in his hand to the siding, where the red paint was smudged, but still glaringly there, and shook his head. ''We're getting nowhere''—he leaned closer to look—''except we're wrecking the finish on the siding.'' He sighed and held out his hand to Bran for the other rag. ''Why don't you go pick up the twins?'' He turned to me. ''Go with him, would you? We took them over to day care this afternoon so's he could rest, but they might as well come home now. Marie's got the car—you'll have to walk.''

''No problem.''

He picked up the can of thinner and looked at the red letters again. "I guess we could paint over 'em."

"We'd better wait a while for that," Bran said.

Mr. Ridley nodded. "They better not plan to do any more." He looked up at the blustery clouds. "I'll just bring a chair out and sit awhile. Nice day for sitting on the porch."

I pulled my jacket up around my neck. "Real nice."

"Let's go," Bran said. We started off, taking the short cut through the cemetery.

"You still hurting?" I asked, as we headed up the gravel road. He was still limping a little.

He shook his head. Then shrugged. "Some."

"You look a little better."

"Thanks."

"Did you see that TV show this morning?"

"Yeah." He walked on a few steps, then stopped. "There's one thing wrong with that inherited psychosis theory. The prosecution's doctors say my father isn't crazy." He made that short, sharp sound that passed for a laugh and started walking again. "He's something, they say. But not crazy."

"Do you ever wonder—" I started. But I couldn't go on, couldn't ask him straight out if he was afraid of turning out like his father.

"What?"

"Nothing. Never mind." I left the road that curved around to the right and started across the grass between the gravestones, toward the gate on the other side. After a few steps I realized he hadn't come with me. I turned back to see that he'd stopped where the browning lawn met the gravel.

"I'll stick to the road," he said.

I hurried back to join him, remembering his back-yard. Bodies under grass. "Sorry. It's just shorter—"

"I know." He stepped over a puddle. "Did you mean do I ever wonder if I'm a bad seed?"

I nodded.

"I killed a bird once." His voice was so low I had to strain to hear. "It had been chewed by a cat. It was going to die anyway, so I wanted to help it."

Bran stopped walking and stared down at a drift of leaves at the edge of the road. The wind gusted around us and I shoved my hands farther into my pockets.

"I can still feel that body in my hand when I think about it. I don't even know what kind of bird it was. It just had that brown fuzz still, instead of feathers. And blood all down the front. Its heart was beating so fast I couldn't have counted the beats. Like an engine idling too high. It was so little. So light. I thought I'd just twist its neck. You know, a quick twist and it would all be over. Easy."

He fingered his earring and looked up, then, and past me across the stones. "I didn't—couldn't—twist hard enough. I don't know why. Weak as it was, it tried to get away, and I couldn't make myself do it hard enough. It kept looking at me with those bright, black eyes. I tried five times before I felt the bones break under my fingers. By that time I was crying. I probably hurt it a lot more than if I'd just left it to die. It was only this baby bird. But one minute there was that warm, soft body and that heart beating away and those eyes. Then nothing. Just nothing. I threw it in a trash can and went home and washed my hands. And tried not to think about it."

Bran started walking again, his limp more notice-able than before. "Sure, I wonder about him and me.

But when I remember that bird, I know nothing in the world could make me kill again. I'm *not* like—'' He paused, and when he spoke again the tone of his voice sent a chill through me. ''Like that man in the jail cell in New Jersey. I'm not.''

Rain started spitting again, so we picked up the pace as much as Bran's limp would let us.

When we arrived at the day-care center, Kipp and Keith came roaring out onto the porch and dragged us in to look at the art work they'd been doing. ''This is you, Bran,'' Keith said, pointing to a crayoned purple circle with arms and legs and a huge head with a large black circle where one of the eyes should have been. ''And those're the jerks that beat you up.'' Squeezed into one corner were a bunch of smaller people, looking a little like two-ball snowmen. ''And here's Super Keith, coming with a big gun to blow 'em all away.'' Above the purpose figure's head there was a smaller head, attached to a big red triangle that must have been a cape. Sticklike hands jutted out from the cape, and perched at the end of the hands was an enormous black banana-looking gun, with black dots and red lines coming out of the barrel. ''I'm not done yet,'' he said. ''I gotta put in all the blood.''

''Mine's done,'' Kipp said, pulling Bran over to his paper. ''See? Dinosaurs. Them *Tyrannosaurus rex* kind with the teeth. They're to walk to school with you when you go back. If anybody wants to fight, they'll chomp 'em!''

Bran held up Kipp's drawing, looking at the two green ovals with legs and tiny arms, the heads not much more

133

than jaws full of huge red teeth. "We could use these guys to stand next to the house, Kipper."

"They'd be bigger than any old house," Kipp said.

"Big doesn't count," Keith scoffed, "if they don't have guns."

"Maybe if you're being enough, all you need are teeth," Bran said. "Can we take these home with us?"

"We made 'em for you," Keith said. "You can put 'em up on the wall by your bed."

We had just started home, the boys stomping along ahead of us, brandishing their rolled-up pictures like swords at imaginary enemies, when Bran glanced back over his shoulder and put his hand on my arm.

"What?" I asked.

He leaned closer. "Someone's behind us, trying to stay out of sight. I saw him as we came out, standing behind the porch of the next house. He just ducked behind a hedge. Looks like Ritoni."

I looked back, but didn't see anyone. "Where Jerry is, Nick is."

Bran shook his head. "I think he's alone. We can check when we cross Broad."

My throat felt dry all of a sudden, and I swallowed. I was pretty sure Nick was someplace close. The others, too, probably. "We could have trouble."

"Just keep walking."

I tried to think how Jerry had known where we were. "You think he followed us here from your house?"

Bran shrugged. "I didn't see anybody. But I wasn't looking, either."

At the corner of Birch and Broad, we stopped to wait for a break in the fairly steady late-afternoon traffic, and I looked back. It was Ritoni, all right, doing a clumsy job of getting himself behind a tree trunk. I had a feeling he didn't care all that much whether we saw him or not.

"What do you think we should do?" I asked Bran.

"What about?" Keith asked, walking the curb like a balance beam.

"About the space aliens that landed in the cemetery this afternoon," Bran said.

"Ah, there's no such thing as space aliens," Keith said.

"Except on TV," Kipp added. He looked up with an uneasy grin. "You're just teasing us, right?"

Bran pointed down Broad toward the cemetery entrance and I saw what he'd seen. A couple of figures had just stepped back behind the huge brick columns next to the gate. Nick. And Gordon. Matt was probably there too.

"Nope," Bran said to the twins. "This great big flying saucer landed right in the middle of the cemetery this afternoon, and two aliens got out. They're probably in there somewhere right now."

Kipp's eyes got huge, and he gripped his picture with both hands. "You think they're nice ones like Alf?"

Bran shrugged. "What do you think, David? They looked kinda mean to me."

I nodded. "Yeah. Big and mean."

"We'd better go the long way home, guys, what do you say?" They both nodded, their faces solemn.

"Okay," Bran said. "Tell you what. When these next two cars get past, we'll zip across the street as fast as we can, and go that way." He pointed right, away from the cemetery gates. "You two be the front lookouts and we'll be the back lookouts. If you see any aliens, you run for home, okay? As fast as you can. David and I'll keep them busy till you're safe."

135

"What do they look like?" Keith asked, when we were across the street and walking beside the tall iron fence. He kept glancing into the cemetery and walking faster and faster. Kipp was half skipping, carrying his rolled picture cocked like a bat.

"Purple fur," Bran said. "And four eyes."

I glanced back and saw Jerry, waiting to cross the street, waving to the others. "You think they'll follow us?" I whispered.

"Or cut through and be waiting at the back."

All the way around the cemetery, we pretended to the twins that we were keeping a watch for space aliens. Bran and I each picked up a stick—"To knock 'em on the head with," Keith said with satisfaction. To keep my heart from thumping out of my chest, I thought. Gordon and Jerry were following us, staying well back, but not trying to hide. Nick and Matt were nowhere to be seen.

I wondered if Mr. Ridley had been right, if reporting them to the police would have kept them from going after Bran again. At least in the middle of the day. I was glad we'd seen them in time to stay out of the cemetery. Out here there were cars going by. And houses with people in them.

We had almost made it back to the Ridleys' when I looked over my shoulder and saw that Nick and Matt had joined Gordon and Jerry. They had picked up the pace and were closing in on us fast. I nudged Bran, and he looked back. "Hey, you two!" he called to the twins, who were now fully into the game, dodging from tree to tree and jumping out at each other with wild shrieks. "Aliens coming in from behind. See how fast you can get home!"

The twins began to run, and I heard the pounding behind us as the guys started running, too. Keith was moving pretty fast, but Kipp had begun to fall behind, when Bran swooped down on him and snatched him up. His picture fell from his hands and Bran kicked it out of the way. "Get Keith," he said to me.

Kip yelled, "My dinosaurs!" but Bran just kept running. I slowed long enough to pick up the picture then grabbed Keith and carried him, jouncing against my hip, the last hundred yards to the Ridley's porch.

Mr. Ridley stood up from his chair as Bran and Kipp bounded up the steps, Kipp still hollering about space aliens getting his picture. Keith and I were only seconds behind.

We set the twins down, and I handed Kipp his torn picture. 'We're all safe," Bran gasped. "The aliens won't get us here."

Nick had stopped a few houses down and was now sauntering casually toward us, hands in his jacket pockets. The others walked behind him, their eyes fixed on the porch.

"Somebody writed all over our house!" Keith said.

"Go on inside," Mr. Ridley said, his voice stern.

Keith started to object, looked at Mr. Ridley's face, and changed his mind. "Come on, Kipper."

"My picture's all tore up!" Kipp complained as they went inside.

Nick stopped directly in front of the house. Bran was still catching his breath from the run, but he stood very still, looking back at Nick. No one said anything. After a moment, Nick smiled and then turned slowly away and walked on, Gordon and Jerry and Matt at his heels.

"Like a pack of dogs," Mr. Ridley said, and slammed into the house.

Bran stood there, watching, till they turned the corner and disappeared.

CHAPTER 16

AFTER DINNER THAT evening I sat on a crate in the garage and watched Dad carve. For a long time we didn't talk. I just watched as he moved the fine knives with a sure, easy touch, defining the individual feathers on an owl that was part of a walnut totem pole. The huge bird was nearly finished, its claws resting on the head of a completed bear cub, its "horns" seeming to grow out of a roughed-in lynx above. This was a commissioned piece, the totem animals chosen by a man who'd ordered it for the entry hall of his new house.

"Did he choose the owl for wisdom?" I asked finally, more to fill the garage with the sound of our voices than because I wanted to know.

Dad laughed. "These three are his family—he's the lynx, his son's the cub, his wife's the owl. And he did mention wisdom. He also pointed out that owls eat vermin—fur, bones and all."

"We could use some owls around here," I said. "Big ones." I told him about the graffiti on the Ridleys' house. "I gave Molly your advice about staying away from Bran. She didn't."

"That doesn't surprise me."

"The thing is, I didn't either."

Dad didn't say anything. He adjusted the glasses he wears for doing close work, blew on the feather he'd just finished and began another.

"I'm getting to know him. He's okay. What's happening to him—to his family—doesn't make any sense. They haven't done anything. It's crazy."

Dad nodded. "The world *is* crazy, Davey. A lot of the time it is. You can't change that. Best you can do is come to terms with it—one way or another." He put his glasses up on his head and looked at me. "Just be careful. I don't want you to get hurt."

"Depends on what you mean by *hurt*."

"Right now I'm talking about good old-fashioned physical pain. Be careful."

He put his glasses back down and began working again. *Careful*, I thought. That was pretty much what I'd always been. Not exactly what you'd expect of somebody whose totem was a wolverine. "When did you choose my totem for me?" I asked.

"The day you were born. We had names before, but we wanted to meet you before we chose your totem." Dad laughed. "What an argument that was. They could hear us all over the maternity ward. I was this dove person, and my first kid was a boy. I wanted you to be tougher than me, and I didn't know anything tougher than a wolverine."

"I never thought it was exactly me," I said.

"Maybe we should have chosen a beaver. That's what your mother wanted. You know, worthy and industrious."

I thought about that, and laughed. "You think it would have worked?"

Dad blew on the owl again, sending tiny shavings

139

into the air. "No way to know. Anyway, it's too late now. We chose what we chose. Like it or not, Davey, somewhere inside you is that wolverine."

Friday morning, to the accompaniment of the steady chanting from outside, Dr. Towson announced that because home tutoring at the high school level could not be considered equivalent to class and laboratory work, the school board had decided that Bran should continue attending Ridgewood High. "The suspended students will return to school on Monday, and for the first time in the history of Ridgewood High School, I have asked for a police patrol of our halls. There will be order at this school even if it has to be imposed by outside authority."

This was greeted by a roar of derision, but the voice over the crackling intercom system went on. "For those of you who may be considering a boycott, I should remind you once more of the guidelines governing unexcused absences. Whoever hopes to make passing grades this semester should be present on Monday and every day after that."

I hadn't thought things could get worse, but they did. The few neutral voices had vanished. "Bad seed out," the constant chant from outside, was echoed on walls and blackboards. Someone had written PSYCHO LOVER across Mr. Byrd's classroom door. Teachers who had tried to discuss the situation rationally in their classrooms went suddenly silent. They focused on their regular subjects as if nothing unusual were happening around them.

People were saying that the teachers had sent a petition to Dr. Towson asking to have the suspension extended, "in the interests of maintaining order and promoting education."

The connection between me and Bran had finally been made. No one, not Zach Lewis, not the guys from the track team—no one—was speaking to me. If some kids hadn't made a point of pulling back or turning away when I came near, I'd have thought I'd become invisible. I waved to Kristin once, and she ducked into the nearest classroom. Later, in my locker, I found a note from her, telling me that if I didn't keep away from Bran I was likely to find myself in trouble with "the guys." I supposed it was the best she could do.

Molly had more trouble than I did. People just ignored me. They shoved, bumped and tripped her in the halls. That was the day she called what was happening a plague.

"It's like the Black Death," she said at lunch, as we sat at an otherwise empty table. "It would get into a little village somehow—maybe the germ would come on somebody passing through from a city where it had already started—and in a couple of days the whole village would be sick. That's what's happening here. First it was only Nick and his cretins who were infected, and now it's everybody. Even the teachers. Did you hear about the petition?" I nodded. "They say it's not to punish Bran. It's to protect him."

"Oh, sure. That's like saying nobody should use the subway in New York because people get mugged there. Have you talked to Bran? Did you hear about their house?"

Molly set her milk carton down so hard the milk splashed into her tray. "Yes, I heard. I mean it, David, it's a plague." She shook her head. "I thought we lived in a civilized world. Not perfect, maybe, but rational. With laws. And rules. Bran's only been here—how long? A couple of weeks?''

I thought back to the day I'd first seen him. A Saturday. Today was Friday. I could hardly believe how short a time it was. "Not quite three weeks." Three weeks to change everything.

"A plague of hatred. Maybe Collier's totally evil, but what about everybody here? Beating Bran up and spraying hate messages on their house are stupid kid things. But look at all the adults in it now. It's as if they're giving permission for whatever anybody wants to do. What's to stop it?''

I didn't have an answer.

"They talk as if Bran could infect Ridgewood," Molly said, mopping up the milk with her napkin. "Seems to me it's the other way around.''

During last period Towson announced that he was turning down the teachers' petition to extend the suspension. By the time school was over for the day BAD SEED OUT was spray painted on the windows of his car and all four tires had been slashed.

I worked from three to nine that night. When I got off, the night was dark, the sky choked with clouds, the wind gusty. As I started home, I kept looking over my shoulder into the moving shadows the trees were throwing across the sidewalk beneath the streetlights, half expecting to see Jerry or Gordon—or Nick. I knew they'd have no reason to follow me, not while I was alone, but I couldn't shake the feeling that they were out there somewhere. They hadn't been able to play in the football game that night. No telling what they'd be doing.

Passing the cemetery, I thought again about the way Nick had stood there in front of the house, looking at Bran. And I decided to go over to the Ridleys' before I went home, to see how he was doing.

Once I was inside the cemetery and away from the streetlights, I could barely see the road. I put on as much speed as I could in the darkness, anxious to be out of there, away from the sound of the wind in the leaves, the darker shapes in the darkness that were the headstones, the idea that someone might be following me.

I heard the chant long before I reached the back gate. "Bad seed out! Bad seed out!" I stopped and listened. There were a lot of voices. More, even, than at school, it seemed. For a moment, I thought of just turning back, going on home. I could check with Bran in the morning. It wasn't as if he was expecting me. But then I thought of the Ridleys, in their own house, surrounded by the kind of hatred I'd felt at the school board meeting. Were the twins there, wishing for dinosaurs and guns? How could anybody explain it to them?

I couldn't stop the craziness, turn back the plague. But if I just chickened out and went home, didn't that make me part of it? If I stayed to the backyards, I could at least get close to the house, see what was going on. And if the chanters were all out front, I could maybe get to the back door.

Sticking close to the bushes that stretched across the backyards, I made my way down the block. When I reached the Ridleys' backyard I crouched against a couple of trash cans. There didn't seem to be anyone back there.

The house was totally dark. There wasn't a light

anywhere. Maybe they'd gone, I thought. They could have gotten out the way I'd gotten in, and the mob in front wouldn't have known.

Staying low, I crept up onto the back stoop and knocked on the door. The chant from out front was so loud, I could hardly hear the knock myself, so I knocked louder. Nothing. I pounded with my fist, and this time saw a curtain move in the kitchen window. I backed up a little so whoever was inside could see me in the pale light from the windows of the house next door. The curtain moved again.

"It's me, David," I said, my mouth close to the door. "David Watson."

After a few seconds I heard the lock on the door, and it opened a crack. "You don't want to be here," Bran said.

"You're right about that. But since I am, can I come in?"

He pulled me inside and then slammed and locked the door.

"Have you called the police?" I asked.

"Three times. They came by earlier, when there were just a few people out there, and told them to keep the noise down. The neighbors were complaining. Then they told us—*us*—not to provoke a confrontation. So much for police protection. Molly was here then. She called her folks and they came over and took Aunt Marie and Angela and the twins over to their house. Good thing. A while ago they started throwing bricks."

I followed him through the kitchen and into the small living room. A little light, not much more than a softening of the blackness, came from the streetlights outside. "Can't you turn on a light?"

"Damn near got a brick in the head when we had a light." Mr. Ridley's voice came from my left. Peering into the gloom. I could just make out his figure in the bulk of an overstuffed chair.

"No sense giving them something to aim at," Bran said. Staying behind the curtains, he looked out. "Looks like there are more coming all the time."

"The football game must be over," Mr. Ridley said.

"And we're the after-game party. Terrific town you got here." Bran's voice was bitter. "My aunt got fired today."

"Fired? For what?"

"Nobody'll come into the diner while she's there. They sold one cup of coffee all day."

"Rutkowski claims he's too small to survive a boycott," Mr. Ridley said.

"Yeah. His customers would all be back in twenty-four hours if I left town. So would Aunt Marie."

A shattering crash startled me so that I nearly fell over the footstool in front of Mr. Ridley's chair. Something heavy thudded against the wall behind me and glass clattered to the floor all around.

"You'd better get down," Bran said. "As long as you're in line with a window, they could get you even if they can't see you."

I lowered myself to the floor in front of the couch, aware of the crunch of broken glass under me. The whole thing seemed unreal. This was the town I'd grown up in. We'd never even had to lock our house. "We should call the police again."

Mr. Ridley snorted. He pushed himself to his feet and started for the kitchen. "I'm calling Marie to let her know we're still here."

Bran moved from his place near the window and joined me on the floor. "Before we took the phone off the hook some guy called to say they'd get me out of here any way they had to do it. He mentioned a bomb, specifically, in case I didn't get the general threat. You might not want to hang around very long."

While Bran was talking, I noticed a pale, flickering light reflected on the wall behind Mr. Ridley's chair. "Is that fire?" I asked. My throat was so tight I could hardly get the words out. Bricks I could handle. Fire was something else.

Bran pulled himself up so that he could see out over the back of the couch. "It's fire, all right," he said. I waited for him to go on, to tell me what they were doing, or suggest we run. Something. He seemed paralyzed there.

"Bran?" I asked, finally. "What is it?"

Still he didn't answer. I moved up next to him and looked out. People lined the sidewalk, chanting. In front of them several figures moved around a bonfire in the middle of the yard. One of them was holding a long pole, from which dangled a dummy, dressed in a shirt and jeans, its head dangling to one side. Pinned to the head was a photograph. The others held burning sticks in the air. The flames and smoke of the fire rose and then flattened as the wind gusted. As the man with the dummy moved through the light, I could see that the picture on the dummy's head was the photo of Joseph Collier from the cover of *Life* magazine.

"It's all wrong," Bran said, his voice flat. "It needs a suit. A suit and tie."

"Burn, psycho, burn!" someone shouted. Almost

146

as if it had been rehearsed, the crowd changed their chant.

"Burn, psycho, burn! Burn, psycho, burn!" they yelled as the two with the torches touched them to the dummy's legs.

"Mr. Ridley, call the fire department," I yelled. "They *have* to come!"

The flames began burning upward while the dummy jounced up and down in a wild, jerky dance.

Where his shoulder touched mine, I could feel Bran start to shake as the flames consumed the dummy, bits of burning cloth and stuffing falling to the grass. The flames were licking the photograph then, crinkling the edges and turning them black. A gust of wind caught the flames. Photo and head seemed to explode, bursting all at once into a mass of fire.

There was a sudden pause in the chant, as if even that mindless crowd had been jolted by the dummy's violent end. In the brief silence I could hear Bran's ragged breathing.

The chant wavered into life again as the leader threw his now empty pole onto the fire. Above the sound of voices the piercing wail of a siren began, growing gradually higher and louder.

CHAPTER 17

THE HOOK AND ladder truck roared up the street and screeched to a stop in front of the house, its siren drowning out the chant. Firemen in rubber coats and boots dropped off the truck and people backed off, letting them through. Some of them began edging away as the firemen, seeing no sign of a fire except the bonfire on the grass, began, disgustedly, to kick it apart and stamp out the last flames. When another siren announced the arrival of the police, more people moved off. The cops got out of their patrol car, leaving the red lights flashing, and the rest of the crowd suddenly melted away into the darkness.

Mr. Ridley, who had come in from the kitchen when the firemen arrived, went out onto the porch, and Bran and I followed.

"Took the fire department to get you here, huh?" Mr. Ridley said, as a young-looking patrolman with a pale mustache came up the steps, his hand on the gun at his belt.

"We were on our way here when the alarm was turned in," the cop said, his voice defensive. He didn't sound like a public servant who had come to the aid of a citizen. The other one, a little older, came up and stood slightly behind him. "You were told we'd put your house on a regular patrol schedule. What's happened here?"

Maybe it was the tone of his voice. Or maybe it was watching the mob take off, while the police ignored them. Or the memory of Bran's face when that dummy burst into flame. Whatever it was, I pushed past Bran and stood face-to-face with the first policeman. I had an almost overwhelming impulse to push him backward, into the other, both of them down the steps. "What kind of policemen are you?" I said, my voice shaking. "How come you didn't go after the people who were breaking the law here?"

"David!" Bran said, under his breath.

I felt his hand on my arm, but I shook it off. The policeman's face blurred, and I realized I was crying. "These people are victims, not criminals! They haven't been throwing rocks and bricks and setting fires! Somebody could have been killed here tonight."

"Listen, kid, I don't know who you are or what you're doing here, but—"

"Go inside," Mr. Ridley said. "I'll handle this."

I wiped my face on my sleeve and Bran pulled me back into the dark house. I went, reluctantly.

"Don't start with cops," Bran said, as he pulled the door closed behind us. "It's a fight you can't win."

I followed him into the kitchen, crunching broken glass on the way. Bran turned on a light. "Sit down," he said, and pulled a chair away from the table for me.

I started to sit, and my knees gave way so that I thudded down onto the padded red plastic seat. "I don't know what happened to me. I was just so mad, all of a sudden. At that mob, at the cops for letting them go—''

Bran leaned on the counter. "Turn it off."

"What?"

"That anger. Turn it off. It'll get you in trouble."

I studied Bran's bruised face. Only his good eye, aimed intently at me, gave away any feeling at all. Behind that eye it was as if a fire were burning, hot and steady, but trimmed down. Under control. I remembered what Scott Handleman had called him— *spooky*. "You can't just turn feelings off," I said.

"Sometimes you have to."

"You can't! Maybe I could have kept my mouth shut, but I couldn't have turned off how I felt, how I still feel." I held my shaking hand out above the table. "See? If that guy with the dummy came into this room right now—''

Bran waved his hand, shooing away my words like flies. "If he was alone, you might have a chance—if you were mad enough. But he wouldn't be. He's like Nick. Those guys are never alone. Besides, it isn't just them, it's the whole town. And don't kid yourself. The police are part of the town. You get so mad you take them all on, and you're done."

"Are you telling me *you* aren't mad? Aren't mad now?"

He took a long, slow breath. "I can't afford to be." With both hands he smoothed back the hair that had come loose from his ponytail. His hands, I saw, were shaking, too. "You're wrong about feelings. You can force them down so deep you don't have to know they're there. Sometimes that's what you have to do." He pushed himself away from the counter. "You want some cider? I think there's a little left."

We sat at the table and drank the rest of the cider. Gradually, my hands stopped shaking and I began to feel like myself again. When Bran had drained his glass he leaned forward. "I won't let this get to me. I can't. When they took my father away I said it was a mistake. They had the wrong guy. He wasn't perfect, but he couldn't have done what they said he did." Bran ran one finger around the top of his glass. "Then the digging started."

After a while he went on. "The police think he probably killed dozens of kids. He'd offer to help them—find them a job, a place to live. He was this nice, respectable guy in a suit. Kids believed him."

I stared at the cider ring on the table next to my glass and thought about all the pictures of him. This nice, respectable guy in a suit. "It must have been awful to find out."

Bran nodded, absently, as if what I'd said was too obvious to notice. "You try to go back and find clues—something that might have told you what he was really like. I guess they were there. Little flashes, sometimes, when he'd get mad about some unimportant thing. But nothing you don't see in anybody else. I've never been able to figure it out, how he could have been the man I thought I knew and that other one, too, who did what he did. I mean, I had to accept it, you know? When they found the bodies in our yard—"

I thought of the body bags being brought from the place where Bran's fort had been, and my stomach twisted.

"I never visited him in jail." Bran sighed and straightened up in his chair. "I thought if I changed to my mother's last name maybe that would keep me from being Joseph Collier's son. I don't look like him, I don't dress like him. But it doesn't change anything. I *am* his son.'' He held up his arm. 'It's my blood in here, but it's his, too.''

I looked at my own arm on the table, the veins at my wrist. My blood, just mine.

He looked at me, his right eye nearly focusing with the other. ''He did what he did and I can't change that. But I'm here. Me. I have to figure out who that is. I have a life. I have to figure out who that is. I have a life. I have to do something with it.''

Bran took our cider glasses to the sink, and I thought about Dad, who'd chosen a dove for his totem and a wolverine for mine. Whose eyes looked out of the mirror at me.

Mr. Ridley came into the kitchen then. In the light from the fluorescent fixture overhead, he looked much older than he'd looked that day I'd first seen him—as if years had been packed into days. I've heard that people's hair can turn white overnight. It wasn't like that. His thinning hair was the same dark brown, just touched with gray. But there were circles under his eyes, and the skin of his face sagged, pulling his eyes and mouth down at the corners. He could have been Bran's grandfather instead of his uncle.

''A squad car'll be out there the rest of the night. Keep people away.''

''They should have been there from the start,'' Bran said.

Mr. Ridley ran a hand over his face. ''A lot of things 'should have been.' They were 'too busy.' '' He opened a door next to the refrigerator and took out a broom. ''The glass needs sweeping up. Can't have it

152

there when the twins get back. And I gotta cover the windows. It's cold—"

"We'll do it," Bran said, taking the broom from him. "You get some sleep. You've got work tomorrow."

Mr. Ridley looked at Bran for a moment, then turned away. "Not tomorrow. Things are slack at the shop. I'll go down and find something for over the windows."

I checked my watch. "I'd better call my father and let him know I'll be late."

"Why not stay?" Bran said. "You don't want to go out there alone."

He was right. Nick and the others were out there somewhere. When I called Dad I didn't say much about what had happened, only that the police were watching the house.

"You sure you're okay?" he asked. "There was something on the news about a fire call."

"False alarm," I said. "The house is intact and the cops are on guard. The world's crazy, but I'm fine."

There was a long silence, and I half expected him to say he'd come get me. But he didn't. "Sleep tight," is what he said.

CHAPTER 18

I DIDN'T EXACTLY sleep tight. Every time I closed my eyes, that dummy's head exploded in flames again against my eyelids. I was on the upper bunk in the room the twins shared with Bran, and I probably did get some sleep, but it didn't feel like it. It felt like a whole night, minute by minute, staring into the darkness, turning and twisting and bumping my elbow on the rail that was there to keep Keith from falling out. The cops must have stayed out in front, as they'd promised, because no one came to chant or throw rocks. But the quiet didn't help me sleep.

Finally, when it began to get light, I gave it up. I swung my legs over the side of the bed and saw that Bran, on his bed against the opposite wall, was awake too. He was sitting cross-legged, a blanket wrapped tightly around him. On the wall above his head were the twins' pictures, Kipp's torn and dirty dinosaurs mended with Scotch tape. "What time is it?" I asked.

"Six-thirty."

I yawned and stretched. "I ought to run. You want to go with me?"

"I'd slow you down."

"We can jog. Or just walk if you want." I jumped

down and grabbed my jeans off the lower bunk. "I don't always have to go for speed. I just need to get out—blow the cobwebs away."

Bran threw his blanket off and stood up. "Me, too. It was a pretty lousy night."

"What there was of it. The crazies ought to be in bed at this hour, so we'll have the world to ourselves."

Mr. Ridley wasn't up yet. We had some orange juice, then walked through the gloom of the living room, where the cardboard we'd taped over the windows shut out the light. It was a shock to step outside into the crisp brightness, where our breath puffed white in the sun.

The police car was parked against the curb, and the single cop inside looked asleep, his head against the window. "Eternal vigilance," Bran muttered.

The blackened patch on the trampled grass of the front lawn, and the scattered chunks of burnt firewood, reminded me of the night before, and I didn't know whether it was the memory or the chill that made me shiver. The sun, just over the red and yellow trees across the street, blazed against the deep blue sky, but there was no warmth in it. I blew on my hands to warm them. "Chilly."

"So let's get going.'

Without thinking about where we should go, I started my usual way, up the sidewalk toward the cemetery, at an easy jog. Bran, though he was still favoring one leg, managed to keep up so that our feet hit the pavement at nearly the same time.

"You're pretty serious about running," Bran said.

"I don't know about serious. I just like how it feels.

And knowing I can keep going longer than most people."

"That night at the quarry—how far'd you go?"

We'd passed through the gates by then, angling uphill as the road curved. I laughed, remembering how the others had dropped behind, one after the other. "I went all the way down to the highway. Bruno didn't make it half that far. No endurance, those guys."

The sun lit the maple leaves over our heads so that the air around us seemed almost to glow. Shadows danced on the headstones. I looked at the names carved into them. Thomas. Heroux. Catallo. Some of the names were old Ridgewood names I knew well. They were people whose children or grandchildren or great-grandchildren still lived in town. Bits of their genes were still living. So did that mean in some way they weren't really dead? I wondered where Bran's father would be buried, if he were executed.

"It's a pretty place," Bran said, startling me out of my thoughts. "But I don't like it."

"I used to. Not so much anymore." It was true. Ridge Lawn had been only a nice place to run. Now that I kept thinking of the bodies under the grass, it would never be that again.

Bran went on a few paces, breathing hard, before he could talk again. "Did you ever think that we're all under a death sentence?"

I slowed down and looked at him. He slowed, too. "That's an ugly way to look at it," I said.

"Not so bad. We're free at least."

"And we've got time." I looked at a bouquet of fading plastic flowers leaning against a headstone. "Lots and lots of time." I speeded up again, anxious to get out the other side.

156

We alternated jogging and walking, so Bran could get his breath, and went on for another ten minutes. Then, seeing that we were near Molly's, Bran suggested we stop there. "We don't need to worry about waking anybody," he said. "With the twins there, the whole household will be up. I want to see how they're doing this morning. They were scared last night."

"I can imagine."

"Scared and mad." He smiled. "Keith wanted to get his bow and arrow and start shooting people."

"Sounds like a terrific idea to me."

"The arrows have suction cups on the ends. I don't think he would have been satisfied."

We jogged the last couple of blocks to the rolling lawn where both the tall frame house and the single-story veterinary clinic stood, surrounded by shrubs. Molly, in a tattered terrycloth robe, answered the door almost as soon as I rang the bell, her four dogs milling and jumping around her feet, barking and wagging.

"Bran said you'd be up." The smell of coffee and fresh muffins wafted out to us. Molly, frowning, pushed the dogs back. "What's the matter, aren't you glad to see us?" I asked, as Juno, the Rottweiler, put her huge paws on my chest and tried to lick my chin. I shoved her down.

Molly glanced at Bran and smiled, but it wasn't a convincing smile. "Why wouldn't I be glad to see a couple of sweaty guys on my doorstep at the crack of dawn on a Saturday morning? And me all dressed for company. Come on in, you're letting in the cold."

She led us through the front hall, the dogs still milling around us, Muttsy, in spite of her missing leg,

157

holding her own with the others. In the sun-filled kitchen Mrs. Pepper, in a red velour robe, and Mrs. Ridley, dressed, her purse on the floor beside her, sat at the round oak table, coffee mugs in front of them. "Look who's here," Molly said. Her voice was unnaturally cheerful.

"I wanted to see how the twins were doing," Bran said, patting Juno's head as the others circled him, tails waving. Mai-tai, the one-eyed Siamese, came out from under the table to join the group. "They must be crazy about all these animals. Where are they?"

Mrs. Ridley and Mrs. Pepper exchanged glances, and Mrs. Pepper stood up hurriedly. "Why don't you two join us for some breakfast? We just took some muffins out of the oven. And how about coffee? Molly, get mugs for the boys." She took a pan of muffins from the stove and set it on the table. "Sit, sit!"

It wasn't like Mrs. Pepper to play fussy hostess. Mostly, she expected me to help myself, which wasn't a problem, since I'd practically grown up in her kitchen. But I sat, and Bran joined me, while Molly got two mugs from the cupboard and Mrs. Pepper poured coffee.

"Was there any more trouble last night after Frank called me?" Mrs. Ridley asked.

"Just more of the same," Bran said. "They broke most of the rest of the windows. The police came, finally, and the people left. You don't want to see the front of the house." He didn't mention the dummy or the fire.

Mrs. Ridley sighed. "I hope our insurance covers the windows. And the painting." She looked up at

Mrs. Pepper. "Frank says we'll have to have the house painted. The spray paint won't come off. Funny, that's why we got the siding, so we wouldn't have to paint anymore."

I took a muffin and buttered it. Mrs. Pepper went to the refrigerator for some jam and set it in front of me. There was a tension in the room I couldn't put my finger on. Something was wrong, something everybody knew but Bran and me. The muffin was warm, but I hardly noticed the flavor of the bite I'd taken.

"So, where are the boys?" Bran asked, taking a sip of his coffee. "They can't still be asleep. And where's Angela?"

No one said anything. I took another bite of muffin and Bran, looking from his aunt to Molly's mother, put his mug down. Molly picked Mai-Tai up and buried her nose in his fur. "What's the matter?" Bran asked, finally.

"They're gone," Mrs. Ridley said, her voice so low it was hard to hear.

"Gone? You mean they went home already?"

Mrs. Ridley shook her head. "Angela took the twins to a friend's place in Utica. She's coming back this evening to pack up their things. We tried to call last night, but the phone—"

"What do you mean, pack up their things?" Bran asked. "You don't mean she's taking them there to stay!"

The only sound in the kitchen was the low rumble of Mai-Tai's purr. Mrs. Ridley carefully wiped up a coffee spill with her paper napkin, then folded the napkin into a tiny square. She nodded.

"But why?"

"She's afraid, Bran."

"But the police came, finally," Bran said. "They left someone there all night. Nobody's going to hurt the boys while the cops're on guard. And I'll watch them the rest of the time. You told her that, didn't you? I'll watch them!"

Mrs. Ridley looked down at her hands. "That's just it. It isn't only the rock throwers." She cleared her throat. "She's afraid to leave them with you, Bran."

Bran stared at her, his bad eye angled wildly off. The color had drained from his face and the bruises looked darker than ever. "She's afraid of *me*?" he said, his voice little more than a whisper.

"I tried to talk to her." Mrs. Ridley looked up at Mrs. Pepper. "We all did. She says she likes you, and if it were just her, she wouldn't even think about it. But you know how much she loves the twins—"

"Yeah—I know," Bran said.

"She says we don't know—even *you* don't know— whether those doctors are right. Whether you have something of Joseph in you somewhere that might come out someday."

Bran's voice was flat. "She thinks I'd hurt Kipp and Keith?"

"She's afraid you wouldn't be able to help yourself."

Mrs. Pepper put her hand on Bran's shoulder. "She's very young, Bran, and frightened for her children."

"Dad tried to tell her there isn't any evidence for that bad seed thing," Molly said. "She said that didn't mean it couldn't be."

I looked down at the plate in front of me. I had broken my muffin into crumbs. Mrs. Ridley spoke again, and I saw that there were tears on her cheeks. "Try to understand. She loves those boys more than anything in the world."

"So do I." Bran pushed himself away from the table and got up. "Thanks for the coffee," he said to Mrs. Pepper. "I've got to be going."

Molly put down the cat, as if to go to the door with him, but he shook his head at her and hurried out, the dogs following. When she heard the door slam, Mrs. Ridley put her head in her hands.

I stood up to go after Bran. "Let him go, David," Mrs. Pepper said. "Let him go."

CHAPTER 19

NOT LONG AFTER Bran left, Molly drove Mrs. Ridley home and I went along, squeezed into the back of the Civic. Bran and his uncle were nailing plywood up over the front windows when we got there. When Molly asked, Bran said he was okay, but he didn't look okay. He was moving in a kind of slow motion, the way he had after the beating. Molly offered to stay and help, but he told her to go on home. I couldn't even offer, because I had to work from eight to four. The police had gone, but Mr. Ridley said they'd promised to come by every couple of hours to check on things.

Molly dropped me off at home, and we agreed to go back to Bran's when I got off work. "Nothing's going to happen during the day," I said, partly to reassure her, partly to reassure myself.

"I just don't think he ought to be alone."

"He isn't alone. His aunt and uncle are there."

"You know what I mean."

All day as I bagged groceries and dragged carts in from the parking lot, I found myself looking at the people coming and going from the store. Had any of them been there last night?

I watched mothers trying to keep their kids from taking candy bars off the shelves by the checkout line, fathers telling kids to stay away from the gum and prize machines, people with food stamps, guys buying beer and potato chips, elderly couples using handbaskets instead of carts. Just people. The kinds of people I'd seen around Ridgewood all my life and felt comfortable with. Safe with.

By the time my shift was over and Molly had come to pick me up, I'd almost convinced myself that the people who'd cheered the burning of the dummy must have come from someplace else. I wanted to believe that there was something different about people like that, something you could see. Something that could warn you.

"Have you talked to Bran since this morning?" I asked, when I got into the car.

Molly shook her head. "I called a couple hours ago, and Mrs. Ridley said he was taking a nap, but she hoped we'd come over later."

The Ridleys and Bran were in the kitchen when we got there, and all the lights were on. Even the windows that hadn't been broken the night before had been boarded over "just in case," Mr. Ridley explained, so it was like night inside. The blankness of the windows, not being able to see out, gave the house the feeling of a prison. I didn't like it. Didn't like the feeling that if the mob came back, there was no way to see what they were doing.

"I'm glad you're here," Mrs. Ridley said, as Molly and I joined her at the kitchen table. "Maybe you can help us talk some sense into Bran's head. He's talking about going back to New Jersey, letting the state put him back into foster care.''

Bran was sitting on a kitchen stool, his hands clasped around his knees, his shoulders hunched. His bad eye wandered as he looked up at us, as if he were too tired to control it at all. ''I survived it before.''

''It was bad then, and it would be worse now, with the trial.''

''It's the only thing that makes any sense. I can't stay here. Look what it's doing to you. Your house is wrecked.'' He turned to his aunt. ''You've lost the job you had for ten years.''

''Maybe it was time for a change,'' Mrs. Ridley said. ''You're family.'' She looked at her husband, who was leaning against the counter, his arms crossed, staring down at the floor. He didn't look up. ''I'm not going to send you back to stay with strangers.''

''We're leaving Ridgewood,'' Mr. Ridley said, his voice tight and hard. Bran turned to look at him. ''We decided while you were sleeping. We'll sell the house and find someplace else, some other town. Start over.''

Bran slammed his fist against the wall and we all jumped. ''You can't do that! Your friends are here. Your lives are here!''

Mr. Ridley shook his head. ''Looks like that's changed. I didn't see any friends here with us last night.''

''Our lives will just have to be wherever *we* are,'' Mrs. Ridley said.

''But your jobs—'' Bran said.

''There are restaurants in other towns. And Frank's been thinking about a garage of his own for years.''

164

Mr. Ridley made a sound in the back of his throat that could have been agreement. Or something else.

"We'll manage." Mrs. Ridley reached out and put a hand on Bran's head. His face, as always, was still, but pale, the bruises turning yellow at the edges. She brushed a strand of hair back. "I had a sister once who got mixed up with the wrong man and before she figured that out, she had you. She was too young to know what to do—younger than Angela—so she ran away. There wasn't a thing I could do then. We lost her, and I thought we'd lost you, too. But you're here now and that's how it should be. I'm not going to lose you again. You're not going to strangers."

"You think it'll be better in any other town?" Bran asked. "As soon as they find out who I am—"

"We'll cross that bridge when we come to it," Mrs. Ridley said.

"I can go some place by myself. Get a job—"

"And end up on the streets?"

Mr. Ridley overrode his wife. "Understand this, Bran. With or without you we're leaving Ridgewood. I won't stay here after this."

Mrs. Ridley turned to us. "You tell him he's got to go with family."

"You can't go back to where the trial is," I said.

"He's right," Molly said. "And you can't live by yourself."

Bran nodded, wearily. "All right. But I'm not making any promises. If we go somewhere else and this starts happening again—"

Mrs. Ridley looked at the clock over the stove. "Angela will be here pretty soon to get the twins' things."

This time Bran's face registered his feelings, and I

looked away. It hurt to look. "I don't want to be here," he said.

"Come to my place," I offered. "I'll fix dinner, and you can meet my dad. You come, too," I said to Molly.

Dinner that night was like a time out. A sort of vacation from everything that had been happening. Dad was in the workshop when we got there, and while Molly and I made chili and a salad, he gave Bran the grand tour of the Watson wood sculpture and totem museum, inside and out.

By the time they came in to eat, Dad was talking to Bran as if they were old buddies. He'd been expounding his philosophy of totems, and apparently Bran was hooked. As we ate, Dad talked about the Northwest Indians, who'd invented totem poles, and how some would choose a totem to be their guardian spirit.

He gave us more of his philosophy than I had ever heard before. He had added plenty of his own ideas to the old Indian traditions, and mixed in a little Hinduism, a little Buddhism and a lot of modern art. But basically he'd kept that guardian spirit idea.

Everybody had a link, he said, with an animal. More than one. Everything people were, an animal was, too. He talked about how a person's totem could influence his life. Whenever he'd stop to concentrate on his chili, Bran would ask him a question and get him started all over again.

Once, when Dad was telling about the woman who had insisted he make her a garden totem that included the grizzly bear she'd chosen as her own symbol, her husband's eagle, and their pet Pekingese—"not a

symbol for him, but a carving of the actual dog"—
Bran actually laughed. A real laugh. Molly jabbed her
elbow into my side, and I nodded. It was as if everything outside our house had disappeared for a while
and the four of us were the only people in the world.

"You should have seen the finished piece," Dad
said, waving a saltine in the air. "I did it just the way
she wanted it. Bear on the bottom, eagle on the bear's
head, and on top of the eagle, that Pekingese. Awful
little dog, the real one was. Nipped me three times
before we were done. So I carved a flea into the base
of its tail. Out there in a garden somewhere is a
wooden Peke with a wooden flea forever biting its
rear end. I like to think for the rest of its life that
wretched beast had an itch it couldn't scratch."

For a while Bran was the way he always was with
the twins—open and relaxed and easy. When dinner
was done, Molly and Bran and I got into a mock
battle over who'd wash and who'd dry the dishes. Even
Dad got into it, flicking us with a dish towel, dodging
around the table when we tried to get him back.

Finally, though, the break was over. The dishes
were done, and Dad said good-by and went back to
work. Bran looked outside into the darkness. His face
seemed to close down again. "If you two don't
mind," he said, "I think I'll walk home."

"I'll take you," Molly said. "I don't think it's such
a good idea for you to be out there alone."

"I need some time by myself. To think about what
to do. Uncle Frank and Aunt Marie are at the house
and I'm just not up to facing them right now. Their
lives were just fine here till I came along." He looked
out the window again. "It's nice out. I thought I'd
walk up to the quarry. Climb down to your platform.

Just sit and watch the water for a while. It's so quiet up there.''

"You can't go there," Molly said. "Nick knows about it now."

"Not the platform. Besides, he won't be up there without his car. If I see it, I'll turn right around and come back."

"Why don't you just stay here," I said. "We'll leave you alone, if that's what you want. You can have my room. Molly and I can watch a movie on TV and you—"

"I'll be okay."

"Then let us take you at least," Molly said.

"I want to walk awhile. You know, blow the cobwebs away."

I didn't want to let him go off alone, but I didn't know how to stop him. We couldn't just force him into Molly's car. And he'd made it clear he didn't want us with him.

"You'll be careful," she said. "Promise."

"I'll be careful."

"If you see Nick and the guys, or if the crazies are hanging around your house, you'll come right back here," I said. "And stay."

"Okay."

We walked outside with him. It was clear and surprisingly warm. "Indian summer's coming," Molly said. "And will you look at that moon!"

Full, or nearly full, the moon rode above the trees, throwing so much light that the bushes cast shadows across the driveway. A plane was moving just above the moon, leaving a silver trail behind it. Bran watched it for a moment. "I wonder where it's headed," he said.

"West," Molly observed. "Chicago maybe. With a stop in Pittsburgh."

"Or Detroit," I said.

"I'd take either of them right now."

Molly shook her head. "It might be Cleveland."

"Even Cleveland." He looked down. "I wonder if it would make a difference."

His voice sounded hollow to me, full of such pain that I threw my arm around his shoulder. Embarrassed, suddenly, I stuck a foot out and pretended to be throwing him to the ground. "We can't let this man go to Cleveland!" I said.

Bran pushed me off. "All right, then. I won't go there." He turned and looked toward the garage, where light spilled from the windows. "I'd like your dad to carve me a totem someday. A bird."

"An eagle?" I asked.

He shook his head. "A raven, I think."

I punched him on the arm. "Nevermore, huh? Okay."

"I couldn't afford it, though."

I laughed. "My dad's not into money, didn't you notice? If you want a raven, he'll carve you a raven."

"If he gets a raven," Molly said, "I get a wolf. I've always wanted a wolf."

"I'd have thought a toad for you," I said.

Molly aimed a kick at me and I jumped out of the way.

"I'd better be going," Bran said. "I don't want to be out too late. Aunt Marie'll get nervous. You running tomorrow?"

"Sure. You want to come along?"

He shook his head. "I'll just wave as you go by.

See you.'' He started down the driveway, his hands in his pockets.

"Is it okay if I come over tomorrow after church?" Molly called.

He turned back. "Could I stop you?"

"Nope."

"See you after church, then." He turned onto the sidewalk and disappeared behind the bushes.

"I'd wish he'd stay," Molly said.

Whenever I think about that night, I hear her say that, over and over, like a stuck record. "I wish he'd stay." But he didn't.

Molly and I went back inside and watched an old movie on television. It was just finishing when the phone rang.

It was Mrs. Ridley. "Is Bran there?" she asked.

"No, Mrs. Ridley, he left." Molly turned off the television and came to stand by the phone. "He said he wanted a little time by himself—to think. He was going up to the quarry for a while."

"There's a crowd outside again. I wanted to warn him. The police are here, but I don't want him to try to get through that mob. Did he say when he was coming home?"

I covered the mouthpiece and whispered to Molly that Bran wasn't home yet. "He didn't want to be out so late you'd get worried about him," I told Mrs. Ridley. It had been two hours, I realized. Had he meant to stay that long?

"Well—" Mrs. Ridley cleared her throat. "I'm sure he's all right, but—" Her voice sort of dwindled away.

"How about if we go up and get him? We can bring

him home in Molly's car. Or back here if you think that would be better.''

"Would you, David? I hate to put you out—"

"No problem, Mrs. Ridley."

"And have him call me, would you?"

"Sure." Molly was already getting our jackets. "We'll go right now."

CHAPTER 20

"I HOPE HE'S still up here," I said, as Molly maneuvered the curves of the quarry road. "If we miss him, he'll walk right into whatever's happening at the house."

Molly, concentrating as the car skidded on the gravel, didn't say anything. I remembered how it felt to be inside the Ridleys' house with the windows covered, and was glad we'd be taking Bran back to my house. Maybe we could pretend for just a while longer that things were okay. Just for tonight. And maybe tomorrow. Molly slowed down as we passed the place where the path left the road. "Almost there," I said. "You can pull over just around this curve."

We rounded the curve and she slammed on the brakes as our headlights shone on the back of a rust-spotted Mustang, stopped partway into the weeds. "Nick's car," Molly said. "Damn!"

I felt my hands suddenly go cold, and my stomach tighten. "They must have come after he was already here." Molly pulled up behind Nick's car and set the emergency brake. "Maybe he's still down on the platform, waiting till they go." I shoved open the door, pushing sumac branches out of the way as I scram-

172

bled around the car, trying desperately to think of something we could do besides go in there to face Nick. I thought of what Bran had said, that Nick was never alone. They'd all be here.

Molly was out of the car, rummaging under the seat. "Great! The batteries are shot," she said, holding up the flashlight, whose beam was easily outdone by the moonlight that flooded down around us.

"My fault."

She slammed the door. "I'll take it with me anyway. I don't feel like meeting up with those guys barehanded."

We hurried down the road and stopped where the path led into the darkness under the trees. "We should get help," I said.

"No time," Molly answered.

I nodded, trying to swallow the lump in my throat that seemed to be cutting off my breathing. "Hang on," I whispered, as she started down the path. "Let me find a stick or something." I scrabbled around in the tall grass, and found nothing.

Molly stopped and kicked at something. "Take this," she said, her voice low. "By my right foot."

I found what she meant, a rock she had loosened. I dug it out, and filled my hand with a rough, heavy sense of security. "Okay, let's go."

Moving as fast as we could in the thick darkness, we stumbled along the trail, slipping in the leaves, ducking low branches. As we got close to the shack I thought I heard voices. I put out my hand to stop Molly. "I think I hear them," I whispered.

We stood for a moment, listening. The only sounds were the wind in the trees and the slow murmur of late crickets.

173

"We don't want them to hear us coming," Molly whispered.

We went on, picking our way carefully, until the path opened out onto the quarry rim. The clearing was empty in the moonlight. But a gleam shone through the bullet holes in the old shack briefly, as if someone had moved a light inside. A dark form came out of the trees across the clearing and toward the shack. "Nobody up here," it called. It was Gordon.

"Here either." Nick's voice came from the shack, and the light gleamed again. "Might as well bring the beer."

"It's in the car," Gordon said, pushing through the sumacs toward the shack entrance.

"You want to go check the platform, or should I?" Molly asked, her lips against my ear, when Gordon was out of sight.

"If he's there, he'll know better than to come up now," I whispered. "We could go back to the car."

"We can't leave till they do, in case they find him. You stay here," she said, "And I'll go around to the other side. Get hidden, and wait."

Before I could say anything, Molly slipped off, weaving her way through the underbrush. I could hear Nick's and Gordon's voices now, but I couldn't make out what they were saying. I hoped they'd stay in the shack till Molly got herself hidden, because I was terribly aware of the sounds she was making.

I moved off the path and stood against a tree trunk, the rock heavy in my hand. Bran had probably started for home already, I thought, and we ought to be out trying to find him, to warn him about the mob he was walking into.

The dark bulk of Gordon came back through the

sumacs. "Why don't you get something yourself, once in your life," he was saying. He came out into the full moonlight, started toward me and then stopped. "Is that you, Matt?" He turned toward where Molly had to be by now. There was no sound for a moment. "Matt?" Gordon called again.

"Wh-wh-what?"

I jumped and nearly dropped my rock. The voice had come from behind me, between the path and the quarry rim. I turned and could see Matt, a heavy form with a pale face, moving among the shadows. I froze. Then, as slowly as possible, turned back toward the tree trunk, to cover my face.

By that time, Gordon had gone to find out what was making the noises he'd heard. "Nick!" he shouted. "Come see what I found. The Goblin Girl!"

"Get your hands off me, you slime!" Molly's voice rang across the clearing.

Matt was still coming toward the path. If I moved, he'd see me for sure. I decided to wait till he got past me. If Molly was going to need help, I figured I'd have a better chance if I could surprise them.

Around the edge of the tree trunk, I could see the beam of Nick's light as he joined Gordon. "Well, looky here," he said. "You all alone up here, or you got that psycho friend of yours with you?"

"He's no psycho," she said.

"That's not what I hear. I'm surprised you aren't scared of him. Don't you think she ought to be scared, Gordo? Bad seed and all."

"I'm not scared of Bran Slocum," Molly said.

Matt had gone on past me now, and joined the others. I looked around the tree and saw the four of them clearly in the moonlight and the light of the big,

175

fluorescent lantern Nick was holding. Gordon had a tight grip on both Molly's arms, and she was squirming to get loose. "Looks like *you* are, though, Bruno," Molly said, aiming a kick sideways at Gordon.

"What makes you think I'm scared of him?" Nick asked.

"You must be, the way you gang up on him. You haven't the guts to take him on by yourself."

"Nick Bruno's not scared of anything or anybody," Nick said.

The sumacs behind him moved and Bran stepped out from beside the shack. He was breathing hard, but his voice was steady. "Good," he said. "Because here I am."

Nick spun around and dropped his lantern. It tipped over onto its side, spreading its light at their feet. Bran stood, his legs braced, his arms loose at his sides. His earring glinted in the moonlight.

"Get him, guys!" Nick yelled, and Gordon flung Molly to the ground to go after Bran. Matt, too, started moving toward him, a little more warily. As Molly went down, I started forward. By the time I reached the clearing, Gordon had pinned one of Bran's arms and Nick had punched him in the stomach. Bran's foot flashed up and caught Nick in the groin. As Nick staggered backward, doubled over, Molly threw herself onto his back, hitting at him with the flashlight. Matt was grabbing at Bran's other arm. I yelled and ran at Matt, the rock balanced in my right hand. He turned toward me and I was on him, my hand and the rock slamming against the side of his head.

I gasped, partly with the pain in my hand, partly

with horror at the sound the blow had made. Matt took a step toward me, crashed into my chest and sank to his knees. He grabbed at me and caught my right leg as he went down, throwing me off balance. I fell sideways, the two of us tangled together, and my ankle twisted under me as I hit the ground, sending a searing pain up through my leg. Matt lay against me, curled on his side, both hands to his head.

I struggled to my feet, but my ankle gave way under me, and I fell again. Nick had thrown Molly off onto the ground and was kicking at her as she scrambled backward to get out of his way.

He turned to where Gordon and Bran were locked together, each trying to wrestle the other to the ground. Gordon had Bran by the hair, and Bran's arms were wrapped around Gordon's chest. They careened into the side of the shack and nearly went down together. But they managed to stay on their feet, their struggle taking them crashing into the low sumacs. They were hardly more than gray shapes, locked together in the moonlight.

Molly threw herself at Nick again, but he shoved her roughly to the ground and picked up a heavy stick. "Get off him now, Gordon," he yelled. "He's mine!"

He advanced on Gordon and Bran, the stick cocked like a baseball bat, and when he got close enough, he swung. There was a crack that seemed to echo off the quarry walls and Gordon screamed. "My arm, Bruno! You broke my arm!" He seemed to be trying to pull away, but Bran held on.

Nick didn't stop. He didn't even pause. On top of them now, he swung the stick again and again. The three of them disappeared around the shack toward the quarry's rim. I could hear the stick landing and

Gordon screaming at Nick to stop, to let him get out of the way.

Molly was in front of me suddenly, pulling at my arm. "Get up! We've got to stop him. Get up!" She dragged me to my knees, and while I was still trying to stand, she took off, limping, around the other side of the shack, the broken flashlight still clutched in her hand. I touched my right foot to the ground and found that I could put a little weight on it. Hopping and limping, my teeth gritted against the pain, I headed for the sounds of the struggle. As I came around the shack, Bran, Gordon and Nick were dark figures, silhouetted against the silvery water of the quarry below them. Gordon, one arm dangling, was hitting at Bran's face with the other, trying to get him to loosen his grip, but Bran held on. Nick raised the stick again, tinged with moonlight, and brought it down on Bran's head.

For a moment everything seemed to stop, as if a camera had frozen the frame. Then slowly, almost gently, Bran and Gordon tipped toward the water. There was a sound of rocks sliding as they went over and Nick, too, began to slip toward the edge. Molly screamed. Nick dropped the stick and, as his feet slid from under him, grabbed at the plants that grew along the rim. Whatever he touched gave way, and suddenly he, too, was gone. There was a tremendous splash, followed by a thud as something—someone—hit the platform. Then a heavy, sliding sound and another splash.

I sank to my knees and pulled myself over to the edge, where I could look down into the water. In the moonlight, the ledge was empty. The little tree that had held the door in place dangled, leaves downward, its trunk broken. Ripples and splashes broke the silvery sheen of the moonlight on the water, and I thought I could make out dark heads bobbing against the confusion of reflected light. One, two—only two of them.

Carefully, I turned and lowered myself over the edge, feeling with my left foot for the cracks and steps that led down to the ledge and from there to the rocks below. My eyes blurred and burned, and I rubbed my sleeve across my face. When I reached the broken tree I strained to see those dark heads against the water again. There was a flurry of splashing.

"Gordo," came Nick's voice from beneath the ledge I was on, "is that you? Are you okay?"

There was a gulping, choking sound, and then, unmistakably, it was Bran who answered. "It's me—I'm not—okay." I wanted to shout with relief, knowing he was still there.

The splashes grew louder now, and I could make out Nick, heading in a flurry of awkward arm movements toward the center of the quarry, where Bran was a dark spot, his hands splashing sporadically among the silver ripples.

For a moment, I couldn't believe it. I considered jumping in after Nick, dragging him back so Bran could make it to the side. But he was already too far from me, too close to Bran. Desperately, I felt around the ledge for something to throw, but came up with nothing but small sticks and bits of rock. I threw them as hard as I could, but they only pitted the water with little circles.

"Stop it, Nick!" Molly screamed and something bigger splashed into the water behind him. I looked up to see Molly crouched on the rim. "Let him alone. That's enough!"

But Nick didn't stop. He'd closed with Bran now, and another struggle was going on, punctuated with splutters, coughs and splashes. I was on my feet, getting ready to jump in, when the sounds of the struggle slowed and then stopped. There was a silence, and I became aware of crickets from above and all around, their chirring filling the quarry.

I peered out into the water and saw one head. Just one. There was a feeble splash and the head went down, then came up again, gagging. A hand moved. Then again.

I lowered myself over the ledge and climbed down to the rocks at the water's edge, my ankle sending flashes of pain with every step. Above me, I heard Molly starting down. Another splash, still far from the rocks.

"Help me." It was Nick's voice, choked and desperate. "I can't make it. Help."

I heard a sob and realized it had come from me. My chest burned and I felt tears hot on my cheeks. I crouched by the water and looked out into the shimmering silver. Molly jumped down from the ledge and landed next to me. I rubbed my eyes, clearing them, and saw Nick, about ten feet out. He was moving only a little, his head barely breaking the surface of the water. I took a deep breath that seemed to tear at my throat, and sat down. After a moment, Molly sat down next to me.

Neither of us moved. I'm not sure I even breathed until Nick, too, had disappeared beneath the water, and the moon's reflection, unbroken now, smoothed itself into a silver trail. We sat there, not touching, not talking, for what seemed like a long time. And then we climbed up and went for the police.

CHAPTER 21

MOLLY AND I told the police our story, though I only said that during the fight all three of them fell into the water. I didn't say anything about what happened after that. I guess Molly didn't either. I don't know what Matt told them. But in all the news about it afterward, nobody ever said anything about a fight.

Mayor Mahoney gave a speech the following Monday to "lament the tragedy at the quarry." He said Ridgewood had lost young men with great promise who had been important to its future. He didn't mention mobs or special school board meetings, or the house on Larch Street with the boarded-up windows and BAD SEED in red paint all over it. By the end of the week new No Swimming signs had been put up around the quarry—as if what had happened was a swimming party that got out of hand.

That's how the newspaper handled it, too. They printed yearbook pictures of Nick and Gordon, the "top student athletes" who had drowned, and said that no pictures were available of Bran Slocum, the other victim, who had been new to Ridgewood High School. They never even mentioned Joseph Collier.

It was almost as if the month of October had never happened, except for that "accident" at the end.

Bran didn't have much of a funeral—just the Ridleys and Molly and her parents and Dad and me. Mr. and Mrs. Ridley didn't want to bury Bran in Ridgewood, but there wasn't anyplace else. He was off in a far corner, sort of by himself, a mound of dirt and a little metal marker with his name and dates. Dad and I promised to take care of his grave after they moved. They couldn't afford a headstone, so Dad said he'd carve the raven Bran had wanted.

Nick's and Gordon's parents held a memorial service at the high school, and most of the town turned out. I felt like I had to go. Matt was there, his head bandaged, and Jerry Ritoni, who'd missed being up at the quarry because he'd gone to join the mob at Bran's house instead. Mr. Byrd and Dr. Towson and the woman who'd carried the Kid Killer sign were there. All the kids came, and there was a lot of crying.

A minister read from the Bible and said that in our grief at the loss of "our children" we should be happy that God had taken them to be with him. That was when I walked away. I couldn't think about heaven right then, and who did or who didn't deserve to be there.

The national paper that had started it all reported Bran's death inside, with no picture and just a tiny headline, "Collier's Son Drowns." I guess dead, Bran wasn't a very exciting story.

The Collier trial lasted through November and all the way into January. In late January it ended. Collier was convicted and sentenced to death. There was a front page headline in the paper, but that was all. Nobody in Ridgewood seemed to care much about

Joseph Collier anymore. He was just another story that was happening outside somewhere.

I quit the track team and just about everything else, except work. But I kept running every morning when the weather wasn't too bad. It felt good and clean and alone, the one thing I could almost enjoy. I didn't run through the cemetery very often, but when I did, I always stopped at Bran's grave.

Dad carved Bran's raven out of oak so that it would last. He carved it with its wings spread, looking up. I think Bran would have liked it. Among all those gravestones, the Bibles and the angels, it was certainly different. Bran would have liked that, too.

Molly and I never talked about that night, about Nick and what we did. What we didn't do. I don't think we ever will. We don't talk much at all anymore.

I thought about the plague a lot all winter, whatever it was that had infected us all and turned ordinary people into people who could kill someone—or let someone die. It had all started because Joseph Collier was a murderer, and I tried to figure out what the difference was between him and the rest of us. There was one, I knew that. But I couldn't seem to draw a clear line.

Finally, I decided Molly was wrong to call what happened here a plague. This wasn't something that came from outside. It was inside all of us, whatever it was. And it still is.

Bran ran out of time before he could do anything with his life. But maybe all he needed to do was just be who he was. He never forgot that bird's heart, beating in his hand. I think he would have helped Nick if he'd been where I was that night.

Molly will go on taking in strays and standing up for someone everybody else is against because that's who she is. That part of her is stronger than the part that sat with me on the rock that night. Most times it'll win.

That leaves me. When the new grass was up and the tulips Molly planted on Bran's gave were blooming, I went out there. The sun was shining on the raven, and it seemed almost ready to take off. Bran was just another body under the grass, but I kept seeing him with a twin under each arm, taking them to get Band-Aids for their knees.

And I made a decision. I'm going to save all the money I earn at the store so I can go to college. I'm going to do something with my life, like Bran wanted to—something to stand against what I found inside myself that night. I don't know what I'll do, yet. I just know it will be something that makes a difference.

About the Author

Stephanie Tolan was born in Ohio and raised in Wisconsin. She is the author of many fine novels for young readers including *No Safe Harbors*, *Pride of the Peacock*, and *A Good Courage*. She is also the author of an award-winning nonfiction book for adults called *Guiding the Gifted Child*. Stephanie Tolan lives in Waterford, New York.